The House of Eyes

Thomas Bloor

**Hodder
Children's
Books**

a division of Hodder Headline Limited

For my sisters, Pat and Jen

First published in Great Britain in 2002
by Hodder Children's Books

A Catalogue record for this book is available from
the British Library

ISBN 0 340 84180 X

Typeset by Avon Dataset Ltd, Bidford-on-Avon, Warks

Printed and bound in Great Britain by
Bookmarque Ltd, Croydon, Surrey

Hodder Children's Books
a division of Hodder Headline Limited
338 Euston Road
London NW1 3BH

The House of Eyes

Also by Thomas Bloor,
available from Hodder Children's Books

The Memory Prisoner
Factory of Shadows

1

No moon or stars were reflected in the surface of the water. Night lay heavy on the river. But in the distance, some miles upstream, an unhealthy glow stained the sky a dirty orange: the lights of Pridebridge Town.

A large boat lay moored at the bank. Light spilled from the galley porthole close to the stern.

In the galley, Maddie sat down heavily, causing *The Pridebridge Princess* to rock from side to side. Dark water slopped against the hull of Grandad Lemon's riverboat. Maddie turned her large face to stare at the old man. His question had taken her by surprise.

He was standing in the doorway of the little cabin, his white hair jutting out from beneath an oil-stained peaked cap.

"Was it something I said?" He opened his palms in a gesture of bewilderment.

Maddie, a mountain of a girl, fifteen years of age, filled most of the double seat. Keith, Maddie's younger brother, was squashed into the corner next to her.

Both of them looked from their grandfather to their mother and back again.

"All I did was ask how their father was!" Grandad Lemon said to Maddie's mother. "Just a simple enquiry. What's wrong with that?"

There was a tense silence in the little cabin.

Mrs Palmer was standing at the small stove, behind the table that dominated the centre of the cabin. She swayed slightly on the gently tilting deck, a saucepan of congealing baked beans held in one hand, and tipped her head on one side. Her eyes were wide and round.

"What's the problem?" Grandad said to her. "You've got that face on again. Like a chicken with its gander up."

Mrs Palmer's throat reddened above her nylon polo neck. She raised a trembling finger and pointed it at Grandad Lemon.

"I made a vow," she said, in a low, quavering voice, "a vow . . . mmm, yes . . . never to hear a living soul utter that man's name again as long as I lived!"

Grandad frowned.

"But that's daft!" he said. "How can you vow not to hear something?"

"Never you mind!" squawked Mrs Palmer.

"Well, it's silly," Grandad said. "Listen. Quentin Palmer! Quentin Palmer! Quentin Palmer! There. I've said the dreaded name, you've heard it, the vow's broken, OK? Now tell me what the bloomin' heck this is all about!"

Mrs Palmer put the saucepan of beans down, then picked them up again.

"I shan't! . . . Mmm, yes . . ." she said, and turned her head away from the old man.

"Mum," said Maddie, gently, "it's time. Time we talked about it. Time we told someone. It's no good being a prisoner of the past. I should know," she added grimly.

A few weeks ago, Maddie had left the confines of her family home for the first time in thirteen years. This trip on Grandad Lemon's old riverboat was the only time she had ever left the town of her birth. She had been trapped inside the same four walls by a buried fear, a fear planted in her memory by the evil Mr Lexeter, the sinister Head Librarian who had secretly seized the reins of power in the town of Pridebridge. It had been Maddie, overcoming her fear at last, who had brought about Lexeter's downfall. In doing so she had cured her fear of the outside world. She was determined never to let things lie festering in her memory ever again.

"We'll tell you about our father, if you want us to, Grandad," she said. "We'll tell you about Quentin Palmer. Me and Keith'll tell you, won't we, Keith?" Maddie gave her brother a determined look, silently demanding his support. Keith nodded quickly.

"It all happened while Lexeter was holding you prisoner," Maddie said, "that's why you don't know anything about it. Mum made us promise not to tell anyone, ever. But from now on," Maddie went on, sternly, giving her mother a hard stare, "there'll be no more nasty secrets kept in this family."

Mrs Palmer uttered a furious cluck. The pink flush that had started at her throat had now risen to her cheeks and up to the roots of her wiry, sand-coloured hair.

"In that case . . . mmm yes . . . I'm leaving!" she said, and she made her way out of the tiny cabin with as much dignity as was possible for someone having to struggle past a table, her daughter's knees and her father's feet, while still holding a saucepan of baked beans in one hand.

Keith looked alarmed.

"Call her back, Maddie!" he said. "She might get lost!"

"Don't worry, old son," Grandad Lemon said, "she's only gone out on deck. We're moored about six foot from the riverbank. I can't see her jumping across. She never was much of a one for athletics, your mum."

"Besides," said Maddie, "it'll be easier to tell Grandad what happened without Mum in here. Mind you," she added, smoothing the fabric of her dress across her stomach, "I wish she hadn't taken all the baked beans with her."

2

The Pridebridge Princess shifted on the restless waters of the River Pride. Mrs Palmer stood at the rail, staring angrily ahead. The river was shrouded in darkness. In the cabin, Maddie and Keith were telling the last of the Palmer family secrets to their grandfather.

It all started three years ago, when the noises under the floorboards began. Maddie was twelve years old and still deep in her self-imposed imprisonment. She never left the house. In those days, however, her mind roved freely. She was keen to know all she could, about anything and everything. She scoured every page of the *Pridebridge Exchange*, the local paper from which she had taught herself to read, and she examined the view from every window, the dimensions of every room, the weave of the carpets, the texture of the walls. In later years she would fall into a habit of listless inaction, staring out of her bedroom window for hours on end. At that time, however, she was constantly gripped by a thirst to know all there was about her domain, the place she spent all her time: the Palmer home.

If you looked closely enough, Maddie reasoned, a potted houseplant could be seen as a mighty jungle, a patterned hearth-rug could map out an entire country and a single room could be a vast, sprawling continent. It was just a matter of scale.

The house was Maddie's world. So when the noises began beneath the floors, she paid them the kind of attention that a team of geologists would give the first rumblings of a new, previously unknown, volcano.

One morning, at the breakfast table in the kitchen, with a spoonful of Mrs Palmer's glutinous, grey porridge halfway to her lips, Maddie suddenly hissed, "Shhh! Quiet, Keith!"

Keith, picking nervously at half a slice of bread and margarine, and already as silent as a boy could be, looked up at his sister. There she sat, one large hand raised, fingers spread, demanding silence, her head on one side, listening.

"Blast! It's stopped!" Maddie said, after a lengthy pause.

Keith let out a long breath.

"Didn't you hear it?" she went on, accusingly.

"I'm not really sure this time," Keith mumbled. "But, if there is something under the floor, whatever it is, I don't think we should tell Mum."

Their mother was out on the staircase, sorting through the cardboard boxes and plastic buckets that crowded every step, looking for a new scouring pad. Mrs Palmer had a morbid fear of cupboards. She refused to have any in the house. Her alternative storage methods were unusual, to say the least. Maddie and Keith, however, were well used to their mother's ways. But as usual, Maddie was less inclined to be sympathetic than her brother.

"Why on earth shouldn't we tell her?" Maddie snorted. "If we've got rats under the stairs then she needs to know about it."

"It's just . . . you know . . . because of . . . the burglar," Keith stammered.

"I suppose you're right." Maddie gave an irritable sigh. "Lately she's been even more of a nervous wreck than usual."

Three weeks previously, the house had been broken into. While the family slept, a robber had clambered through the fanlight window in the downstairs front room. He had crept about, lighting his way with matches, which he abandoned as they burnt down. In the morning they found a trail of tiny, blackened matchsticks on the front-room carpet. Maddie had made detailed sketches of this evidence, along with the open fanlight and the smudged footprint on the windowsill.

She was enthralled by the break-in, and had thought of little else until the noises under the floor had presented her with a new facet of the life of the house to brood upon. The burglar had climbed in and out again through the same front-room window. He had not investigated any of the other rooms. At first, it seemed as if he had taken nothing. But one thing was missing. It was a silver picture frame containing the only photograph Mrs Palmer had of the children's father, Quentin.

The break-in had horrified their mother.

"Imagine!" she chittered. "A burglar! Coming in, creeping around, looking at our room! Mmm, yes . . . it makes me come over all peculiar!"

She refused, however, to call in the police.

"Ooh no! I couldn't be doing with it, Maddie love, mmn, yes," she said, when her daughter suggested it. "Imagine. Policemen, coming in, creeping around, looking at our room!"

Maddie had sighed, smoothed down the front of her dress and taken another bite out of the chocolate chip cookie she was eating.

There were always plenty of biscuits in the Palmer home. The children's mother brought home packets and packets of them every Thursday, after her weekly expedition to the Saver's Paradise supermarket. She never ate any herself. Keith would occasionally nibble at the edge of a custard cream before putting it down and pushing his plate away. It was left up to Maddie to keep the family biscuit tin from reaching total capacity. She waged war on the perpetual tide of biscuits that arrived each week. It was therefore quite natural for Maddie to turn to biscuits as part of her research equipment when the noises under the floor began.

That morning, she enlisted Keith as her assistant.

"The noises were coming from over by the door, I'm sure of it," Maddie said.

"Out in the hall, I think," Keith mumbled. He always mumbled when he was nervous, and contradicting Maddie made him particularly nervous.

Maddie grunted.

"You're probably right," she conceded, "the floor in here is solid concrete, underneath all the lino."

Mrs Palmer called to them from out on the staircase.

"Scouring pads ... Mmn yes ... I'm all out of scouring pads. I'm just popping round the corner for some new ones!"

The front door creaked open and the sounds from the road outside, followed by a gust of damp air mixed with a hint of raw city fog, infiltrated the kitchen for a second or two. Then Mrs Palmer pulled the door to behind her. There had been the unmistakable breath of the outside world, however, and, brief though it was, it made Maddie shudder.

She shook her head briskly, deliberately shaking off the tremor of fear that the open front door had sent through her. She stood up.

"Right, Keith," she said, "now's our chance, while Mum's out. You bring the biscuit tin."

They went out into the hall and Maddie knelt down just outside the kitchen door. She felt the coarse texture of the carpet imprinting itself on to the skin of her knees.

"The noise was coming from around here, was it?"

"A sort of scraping, scratching kind of noise," Keith shivered. "I heard it yesterday, when I got back from school. It sounded ..." he paused, his forehead

11

wrinkled with thought, "it sounded . . . big," he concluded with a grimace.

"I ran upstairs when I heard it," he added.

Maddie looked at her brother. She saw him hunch his shoulders and shiver.

3

"It's probably just a mouse," she said. "A sweet little mouse. And here's how we'll find out."

Maddie leant forward, her head resting against the wall, and worked her fingers down between the carpet and the skirting board. With a grunt of exertion she wrenched back a corner of the carpet, folding a swirl of the brown and orange flower pattern back on itself. A cloud of dust arose from the disintegrating underlay. It covered the floorboards in a crumbling grey layer. Maddie swept the shreds of underlay aside, raising even more dust. Keith, standing behind her, peering over her shoulder, began to cough.

"Aha!" Maddie glanced up at Keith, a look of triumph on her dust-flecked features, "See? There's a big enough crack between these floorboards. Get some string. Quickly, Keith!"

Keith hesitated. He looked around him, bewildered. Maddie sighed.

"There's some in the big saucepan, up near the top

of the stairs," she said. Keith went pattering away, running up the steps, his tread sounding, to Maddie, as light as rain on a window.

Still kneeling on the floor, she picked up the battered biscuit tin with its scratched and faded views of Canterbury Cathedral, held it firmly under one arm and prised the lid off. She grabbed two biscuits, stuffed one into her mouth, whole, and began picking a hole in the middle of the other one with the long, pointed nail of her little finger, taking care not to let it break into pieces.

More footsteps, like rain pattering on the window again, then Keith was panting at her side.

"Here's the string," he said.

Maddie took the string and poked the end through the hole in the biscuit. She looked at Keith.

"Scissors?" she said. Keith leapt up and ran back up the stairs, delving into the boxes and trays and pots that lined each step. While she waited, Maddie brushed the biscuit crumbs off her lap.

When Keith brought the scissors Maddie cut the string to the required length. She held up the biscuit, looped on to the piece of string. She let it swing a moment, like a conker waiting to be walloped.

"We lower it down between the floorboards, see," Maddie said. Keith watched her gravely. "And we check on it every day. If it gets nibbled we can examine the size of the bite marks and work out what kind of animal is down there."

"It might be mole-rats!" Keith said, in alarm. He had watched a nature programme on television about the furless, sightless and altogether unpleasant-looking rodents. He had not been able to sleep for a week.

Maddie lowered the biscuit through the crack in the floorboards.

"I'm going to need something to fasten the string with," she said. "Keith, Sellotape please."

Keith scurried back to the staircase.

Suddenly there was a ring on the doorbell. A long, confident, nerve-jangling ring. It made Maddie jump. She let go of the biscuit on a string. It slipped through the floorboards and vanished with a flickering swish, like the tail of a terrified mouse.

Maddie knew her mother never rang the bell. Mrs Palmer almost always had a key and on the few occasions she forgot it, she would push open the letter box and call in to her children: "It's only . . . mmm yes . . . me!"

Maddie turned and looked along the hallway. At the front door, a tall figure could be seen, standing outside on the step and silhouetted against the frosted glass.

"Keeeeith!" Maddie called out in a strangled stage whisper, a quaver of fear infecting her voice. The thought of some unknown person from the outside world, waiting on the front step for the door to be opened, filled her with great unease.

Keith, up on the stairs, stared down at his sister from between the banisters, his eyes as round as those of a field vole caught in the shadow of a hawk.

"Don't open it!" Maddie mouthed up at Keith. He turned to look towards the front door and let out a tiny gasp. Maddie heard the clack and rusty squeak of the letter-box flap being lifted. She quickly slid herself back against the wall, carpet burns stinging her bare knees. She waited, her heart thumping. Perhaps this was just the postman, or someone delivering an advert for double-glazing. But, if so, why had they rung the bell?

There were no further sounds from the hall. Keith was crouching on the stairs, still as a mouse. Maddie leant slowly forward until she was looking at the front door. Immediately, she let out a yelp of alarmed surprise and threw herself backwards again. The letter-box flap was being held open by two pink thumbs. A pair of light blue eyes, framed in the narrow opening, met her gaze in an unblinking stare.

4

Up on the stairs, Keith jumped, startled by his sister's sudden cry. His elbow nudged an empty cereal packet and a pair of Wellington boots. The packet tipped, the boots flopped, top over heels, and suddenly an avalanche of shoes, boxes, saucepans and plastic bowls was tumbling down the steps. Maddie watched her brother desperately flailing around, trying to hold back the flood of household items. She sat with her back to the wall, frozen to the spot. The rucked-up corner of carpet by the kitchen door was just inches from her foot.

"Hello? Hello?" a man's voice, deep and melodious, called through the letter-box.

Maddie froze, but then a surge of relief flooded over her. An indignant squawk in the background announced the return of Mrs Palmer. Maddie no longer had to feel that she was in charge of the house. But her relief quickly turned to alarm when she heard her mother's voice raised in a strangled screech.

"Ooh my Gawd! It can't be!"

Maddie looked up at Keith, frozen in surprise on the stairs. Then there came the indistinct voice of the man on the doorstep. He had evidently turned away to face Mrs Palmer. Although his words were unclear, his voice had taken on a concerned tone. They could hear the name "Valerie" being repeated. Keith and Maddie exchanged boggling glances. They knew that Valerie was their mother's name, but they had never heard anyone use it.

With curiosity overcoming her nerves, Maddie peered along the hall once more, just in time to see the letter-box snap open again. A mouth, topped by a pencil-thin moustache, the lips crimson and full, the teeth straight and unnaturally white, appeared in the frame. The mouth spoke.

"Quick, children! Your mother has fainted! Open this door at once, I need your help!"

The voice was full of urgency, but still had a rich, musical quality to it, as if the speaker was more concerned with the sound of his voice than the meaning of what was being said. Maddie had to think for a split second before she took in the facts. Her mother was lying outside on the front path. Even so, the thought of opening the front door was, to Maddie, a terrifying prospect. She stayed where she was.

It was Keith who picked his way through the heaps of Wellington boots and cooking pots, now scattered at the foot of the stairs. He turned the worn door handle and pulled. Then he jumped back and stood on the bottom step while the door swung slowly open with a shuddering creak.

The mist had thickened outside, shrouding the street in pale grey gauze. The derelict building across the street loomed like a bald cliff-face, colourless and featureless in the obscuring fog. Maddie shrank back from the open doorway but could not tear her eyes from what she saw there.

On the doorstep stood a tall man in a pale grey raincoat. He wore a wide-brimmed hat, tipped at a rakish angle. His dark lidded eyes were light blue and unblinking; a pencil thin moustache graced his upper lip. And he was carrying Mrs Palmer!

She lay, draped in his arms, one slipper still on her foot, the other lying on the front path, her pop-socks all wrinkled around the ankle and her itchy woollen coat bunched up in front of her face. She was clutching a packet of scouring pads tightly in one hand.

"Stand back!" commanded the man. His voice was like an enormous gong, softly struck with cloth-covered beaters. Neither Keith nor Maddie were anywhere near the doorway. After a dramatic pause he strode forward, deftly manoeuvring so as not to crack Mrs Palmer's head against the doorframe. He stood on the doormat and looked at Keith, who was shifting from foot to foot on the cluttered stair. Then he looked at Maddie, down along the hall, crouched on the ground near the fridge. His light blue eyes held her gaze for what seemed, to Maddie, an uncomfortably long time. Without breaking his gaze, he hooked one foot around the open front door and carefully swung it shut behind him. Maddie felt a small wave of relief as the door closed, despite the fact that a total stranger had just shut himself in the house with the two children and their unconscious mother. At least she did not also have to deal with her own irrational dread of the outside.

Mrs Palmer stirred in the stranger's arms. She lifted her head, her hair jutting out at all angles, and looked blearily around. Then she seemed to realise that someone was carrying her. She looked up and saw the man regarding her closely, his frowning face a study of concern and sympathy.

"Ooh my Gawd," she whispered and her head dropped back. She had fainted again.

"Well, children," the man intoned, "are neither of you going to lend some assistance? Can it be that you do not recognise me? Has it really been that long?"

Neither Keith nor Maddie moved a muscle. Maddie was staring at the man in fascinated disbelief. The angular jaw, the sculptured cheekbones and, beneath the wide-brimmed hat, the stiffly lacquered, dark and shiny hairdo were all features familiar from the photograph in the silver frame that, until the recent burglary, had stood on the front-room mantelpiece. And yet it was still, somehow, a shock to hear the stranger's next words.

"It is I," the tall man said, "Quentin Palmer. Your father has returned!"

5

Maddie's head was still in a whirl. Only a few hours had passed. Too much had happened. The man in the photograph, with his pencil moustache and his startling white teeth, her father, who neither she nor Keith had any memory of ever seeing before, had suddenly returned. He had carried Mrs Palmer over the threshold. He had put her on the couch in the front room. He had bustled around the kitchen, fastidiously brewing a pot of tea.

"Always warm the pot, children," he intoned, sluicing a little hot water from the kettle around inside the teapot, then tipping it out, casually, on to the floor. "To make tea without warming the pot is criminal!"

And then, with the tea drunk and the cups and saucers left unwashed on the kitchen table, he picked up the telephone, unasked and uninvited, and ordered a large takeaway curry for four.

While they waited for the meal to be delivered, he paced around the kitchen, glancing at the walls, the ceiling, the floor, making the occasional clicking noise with his tongue and flashing his white smile at Maddie and Keith. The two children sat in silence, exchanging bewildered looks.

By the time the food arrived, Quentin Palmer had looked through all the pots, jars and containers in the kitchen. Stooping to pick them up, he had then weighed them idly in his hand, unscrewing the lid with his eyes on the ceiling, a look of bored disinterest etched across his features. Some of the jars he glanced inside and then shut hurriedly. With others he did not bother to replace the lid at all.

When he found the money he clicked his tongue twice. It was the money that Mrs Palmer kept for emergencies, inside a Marmite jar in the washing basket. When the curry delivery man rang the bell, Quentin picked up the Marmite jar and strolled out of the kitchen to open the front door.

"Why doesn't he go away?" Keith said, speaking in a whisper.

"I don't know," Maddie whispered back. "Do you think Mum's awake yet?"

"I hope so . . . Perhaps then he'll say goodbye and go!"

"Here you are, my good man," Quentin's voice rang out in the hallway – he was talking to the delivery man – "and keep the change!"

When Mrs Palmer, conscious at last, but still maintaining a dazed silence, joined them in the kitchen to eat, Quentin showed no signs of being about to leave. Maddie had to admit the food was good. She had never tasted a takeaway before. Mrs Palmer believed in home-cooking at all times. She did make curry on occasion, but Mrs Palmer's curries were really the same as her stews, except they were bright-green in colour and had one or two sorry-looking sultanas floating on a thick-skinned surface.

For Maddie then, the takeaway was a new experience. The crimson and yellow rice, the deliciously warm and pliable naan bread, the chicken dopiaza in its rich red sauce and the triangular samosas with their creamy mint and yoghurt dip in a little polystyrene pot; she found all of it delicious.

By the time she had finished her own plateful, plus what Keith did not want of his, Maddie felt a little more at ease with the situation. Her turmeric-stained dress was stretched tight across her stomach. The unfamiliar spices were still dancing on her tongue and causing her mouth to sing.

Since recovering from her fainting fit, Mrs Palmer seemed to have lost the power of speech. She sat at the table saying nothing. She just gazed, round-eyed, at Quentin. He busied himself sharing out the remains of the takeaway, spooning out the curries and sauces from the foil containers, handing round the naan breads and pakoras and remarking on the quality and consistency of the food. Every now and then Mrs Palmer's face would fold into a soppy grin and a watery film would glaze her eyes.

Maddie kicked Keith under the table. He looked up from his half-nibbled naan.

"Look at Mum," she whispered behind one large hand, "she's gone all goo-eyed!"

Quentin had risen from the table and was draping Mrs Palmer's itchy woollen coat about her shoulders to keep her warm. He behaved as if it were a silken gown. Mrs Palmer, still speechless, just tittered, feebly.

"And now, my dear," Quentin said, "a pleasant after-dinner stroll to the local hostelry, where I will buy you a glass of your very favourite tipple, which is . . ." he let the sentence hang, as if in gleeful anticipation of a fond memory.

"Port and lemon!" breathed Mrs Palmer, her face pink with delight.

"Absolutely! Port and lemon!" Quentin cried in chiming tones. "I'm sure our children are mature enough to look after themselves while we're gone. Be sure to bring your purse, Valerie, my dear," he added smoothly, patting his pockets. "I seem to be a little light at present."

Maddie waited until the front door had shut. Then she raised her hands to her face and let out a long, shaky breath.

"Keith," she said, "I cannot believe this! It's the most amazing thing that has ever happened to us. But something's wrong. Something's very wrong. Why didn't Mum ever tell us anything about our father? Why? Why? And how can he just turn up out of nowhere like this? Surely he's not thinking of moving in and living here as if nothing had ever happened? He's a total stranger, for goodness' sake!"

At this point Maddie had to break off as they heard the front door being opened again and Mr and Mrs Palmer came back into the house. Keith's face showed both his alarm at this unexpectedly quick return and relief that Maddie had stopped shouting.

"The fog has dispersed but there's a spot of rain in the air," announced Quentin, "and I forgot my mackintosh. Rain can play havoc with a twill suit, you know."

He gathered up his light grey raincoat from the back of a chair and threw it about his shoulders.

And then they heard it. They all heard it. The noise from under the floor. It was a scraping, scratching sort of sound. It was coming from beneath the floorboards, out in the hallway.

Mrs Palmer goggled, nonplussed. Maddie and Keith exchanged knowing looks. The effect on Quentin Palmer, however, was extraordinary.

"What's that?" he croaked, startled and alarmed, the music gone from his voice in an instant. "What's that noise?" he repeated, louder this time, and harsher.

"For the last time," and now he almost shouted, his voice full of a fearful urgency, "what . . . is . . . that . . . NOISE?"

6

"There's no need to shout," Maddie said. Her voice had a steely edge to it that surprised her. Here she was, standing up to a domineering adult, yet too afraid to put one foot outside her own front door. She folded her arms and glared at Quentin. Inside the house, with the wide world firmly shut out, Maddie was in her own territory. Like all territorial creatures, she found herself prepared to fight tooth and claw to defend her patch.

Quentin looked astonished. Then a flustered look came over him. He pulled a handkerchief from the top pocket of his twill jacket, mopped his brow and staggered slightly.

"I . . . I'm so sorry . . ." he murmured. "I seem to be feeling a little queasy. I think I should sit down."

The tall man took a couple of paces backwards, out through the kitchen door. He sank to his haunches out in the hallway, his back resting against the wall. He looked up at Maddie. She was pleased to see a look of grudging respect in his eye.

"The noise was coming from here?" he whispered, pointing at the corner where the carpet still showed signs of having been recently pulled back.

"Yes," said Maddie, following him out into the hall. "We think it may be mice. Or rats. Why are you whispering?"

"Rats, you say?" Quentin's voice rose. "You could be right!" he went on, leaning over and lowering his face until his nose was almost touching the rumpled carpet by the kitchen door. "Is that right?" he shouted at the floor. "Are you a rat? A big, fat rat? Or are you a tall, thin one? Eh? Eh?" Quentin was yelling at the top of his voice by now, and pounding the floorboards with his fist for emphasis.

A shocked silence followed this outburst. Quentin seemed to realise slowly where he was. He looked up, his face wreathed in sweat, his lacquered hair suddenly looking bedraggled and unkempt.

"I'm so sorry . . ." he said again. The musical timbre had been restored to his voice. "I think I need to go and lie down for a while."

He climbed to his feet and walked slowly upstairs, not even glancing at the heaps of household items littered at the foot of the stairs.

"Leave it to me," he intoned as he went. "I'll deal with the problem under the floorboards . . . Just leave it to Quentin . . . Father knows best . . ."

His heavy tread was still reverberating in the hallway when Maddie thought she heard, from somewhere below her feet, a barely audible wheezing hiss and the faint slither of something large moving away under the floor. What *was* that sound? There was something in the juddering rhythm of it. Maddie shivered when she realised. The sound had reminded her of a smothered cough. Or a stifled laugh.

But the more Maddie thought about it, the more she began to wonder if she had actually heard the sound at all. Keith, still in the kitchen, had stood up at the vital moment, his chair scraping over the lino, burying the sound.

"Did you hear that?" She turned to Keith, who had joined her in the hall, then to Mrs Palmer, who was standing rooted to the spot by the front door, still in her coat. Mother and son both wore the same wide-eyed expression.

"Couldn't very well *not* hear it. He was shouting . . ." Keith said, eyes on the floor.

"I didn't mean *him*!" Maddie said. "I meant . . ."

"Now you two . . . mmn yes . . . mind your manners!" Mrs Palmer interrupted. "Your father's been away."

The children looked at their mother. Seeing their expectant faces, waiting for her to go on, Mrs Palmer suddenly looked flustered and turned her gaze away. She shrank past Maddie and began picking up the boots and boxes that lay around the foot of the stairs, bending quickly and snatching up various items, like a hen pecking for grain.

"Mum," Maddie said, "you have to explain."

Mrs Palmer gave a nervous laugh. "I'm sure I don't know what you mean!" she said.

"Yes you do! Explain about this . . . this so-called father of ours. Where did he come from? Where's he been? What's going to happen?"

"Now listen!" Mrs Palmer, her arms full of Wellington boots and plastic washing-up bowls, glared at her daughter. "He's come back, and that's that. It was always the way of it with him . . . mmn, yes . . . here one minute, gone the next.

"It's been nine years. I've not set eyes on him since before little Keithy was born. I never thought I'd see him again. And he's so different, too!" A dreamy look came over Mrs Palmer. Her eyes suddenly looked glazed and watery. "What a gentleman he's become, just like I always dreamed he would! Port and lemon . . ." she breathed, then fell silent. A plastic beaker full of clothes pegs slipped out of her grasp and scattered across the hall floor. Mrs Palmer paid them no heed.

"Here, Maddie love," she said, pushing an armful of bowls and boots at her daughter, "I must get on and start the breakfast. He'll want something special when he wakes up."

"But . . ." Maddie knew it was useless to argue with her mother. She would begin preparing the breakfast, now that she had got it into her head to do so, despite the fact that it was close to twelve hours away from breakfast time.

"Give us a hand, Keith," she said.

Keith took a pair of Wellingtons from Maddie's arms and stood them side by side on the right of the bottom step.

"It's like I said, Keith," Maddie said, pointedly turning away from her mother, "there's something not quite right about all this. I heard something under the floor just now. And I see what you mean, it did sound big."

Keith paused while stacking six plastic bowls together on the second stair.

"Mole-rats?" he asked anxiously.

"Much bigger than that."

"Giant mole-rats!" Keith said with a shudder.

"Keith," said Maddie, calmly, "will you shut up about mole-rats! I have to think things out." Maddie pressed two large fingers on her forehead and frowned.

"Nothing ever happens to us, as a rule," she said. "I stay in, you go to school, Mum goes to Saver's Paradise. That's about it. But now, all of a sudden, we have a break-in, we have some unknown father turning up out of the blue and we have something nasty crawling about under the floorboards!"

"You said it was a mouse," Keith muttered, resentfully, "a sweet little mouse, you said . . ." He looked down at her, lips pursed, from halfway up the stairs where he was depositing a dented steel saucepan.

"Belt up, Keith!" said Maddie, mildly. "Now to my way of thinking, the oddest of these recent events has to be the arrival of you-know-who." She jerked her head upwards, indicating the first floor, where Quentin was, presumably, lying down in one of the rooms. "Just what is he doing here?" she said, spreading her fingers in a dramatic gesture. A long, grating snore could be heard in the moment of silence that followed Maddie's words.

"Apart from snorting like a warthog," she added.

Keith looked miserable.

"It sounds like he's asleep in my room," he said.

7

Maddie paced the kitchen floor, her plimsolls squeaking on the grubby lino. With one ear she listened for any further sounds from under the hallway floor. With the other she strained to hear signs of Keith and Quentin's return. It was half-past four in the afternoon. They had been gone all day.

First thing in the morning, Quentin had announced that he was taking his children on an outing. Mrs Palmer made no objections, despite the fact that it was a school day and Keith never usually missed a day at River Row Juniors.

The children's mother had been up since five o'clock finishing off preparing the breakfast. The meal consisted of a huge and slippery plateful of fried eggs. Heaps of tomatoes grilled to the point of disintegration, their skins black and peeling, were also served up, along with a stack of fried bread, the cooking of which had covered the kitchen ceiling in a layer of black soot.

Quentin had smacked his lips and made a great show of eating a hearty breakfast, tucking a white cotton napkin into his shirt collar and shaking dollops of brown sauce on to the side of his plate. When he left the table, however, kissing Mrs Palmer loudly on the cheek as he did so, Maddie was surprised to see that he had, in fact, left most of his food.

Mrs Palmer, standing at the sink, a scouring pad in one rubber-gloved hand, her other hand held pensively to her cheek, did not appear to notice. Maddie had long since grown to tolerate even the most indigestible of Mrs Palmer's cooked breakfasts. She steadfastly finished off Quentin's calcified fried slice and tomato mush.

"I never leave the house," Maddie said, between mouthfuls, looking coldly at Quentin. "Not ever."

Quentin, who was standing at the table, beaming down his white smile on the two children, pulled a face full of exaggerated surprise. His eyebrows disappeared up into his stiff and shiny hairdo.

"You'll change your mind, Maddie, when you see what I have here!" and he pulled three lengths of printed card from his jacket pocket and waved them in the air. "Tickets to the zoo!"

"I never leave the house," Maddie repeated slowly. She glared at Quentin. He met her gaze. After a moment he gave an almost imperceptible nod.

"Very well, I'm sure Keith and I will have a good time, eh Keith? An outing with Father should be splendid fun, don't you think? Yes, of course you do. Coat on, then, and off we go!"

Keith shot Maddie a look of horror. Quentin patted him on the head and chivvied him out into the hall. Mrs Palmer left the sink and scurried up and down the stairs, fetching an array of winter clothing for Keith. Then she fussed around her son, kitting him out in a brown woollen bobble hat, a grubby-looking tartan scarf and a pair of stiff grey mittens joined by a length of hairy string. Finally she reached deep into a hidden pocket sewn into the pleats of her skirt and pulled out a worn leather purse. She handed the purse to Quentin.

"Splendid, my dear, and thank you kindly," he chimed, kissing her on the cheek once more. Then, with a cheery cry of "Farewell, ladies!" he bustled Keith out of the front door and was gone.

That had been hours ago. Now, the November sun had disappeared behind the pine tree at the back of the house, and the kitchen was plunged into dusky gloom. Maddie paced back and forth, her eyes wandering aimlessly over the pattern on the lino. The small black-and-white squares were still just about discernible in the growing darkness.

Maddie had long since worked out the complete area of the kitchen floor, using the squares on the lino as a guide. Now, as she paced, she idly calculated the average distance in square centimetres that she covered with each stride. It was one of many such habits Maddie had contrived in order to keep the surface of her mind occupied while she contemplated other things at a deeper level.

But just then, that part of her mind that was not employed in calculation or basic pacing was chafing angrily at the bit, waiting for Keith to return. More than anything, she needed information about Quentin Palmer in order to make any kind of progress in figuring out what he was up to. She was hoping Keith, having spent all day with the man, would provide that information.

At last, two sets of footsteps, one a confident, ringing tread, the other a light pattering, could be heard on the front path. The door clattered open. Mrs Palmer must have given Quentin a key, Maddie realised with a shock. Quentin strode into the kitchen. Chill, outdoor air and a sour reek that Maddie did not recognise, blew into the kitchen with him.

"Let's shed some light on the subject, shall we, Maddie!" he chimed blithely, flicking the wall switch with his elbow. Maddie blinked as the sudden flood of yellow light filled the kitchen. Quentin, looking rather red in the cheeks, was casting around for somewhere to sit. He headed towards the chair next to Maddie's. Maddie got to her feet and walked out of the room without a word.

"Good afternoon to you too, Maddie!" he sang out after her. Much to Maddie's annoyance, there seemed to be a trace of amusement in Quentin's tone.

Keith was loitering in the hallway.

"We need to talk," Maddie said to him. "Now!"

8

"I sincerely hope, Keith, that you've not been making that man feel welcome in this house." Maddie stared coldly at her brother, who made no reply.

They were standing, face to face, in the understairs cupboard. Maddie had not turned the light on. She spoke in a whisper.

"I'm going to need a full description of this outing of yours."

The door was open just enough to allow a thin band of light to cut a diagonal stripe across the bare interior of the cupboard. Mrs Palmer insisted on keeping this storage area free from clutter, despite, or perhaps, because this was the only cupboard in the house she could bear to use. An old hoover lay against the wall, its hose coiled beside it like a sleeping anaconda. On the back of the door a selection of limp yellow dusters hung on a row of bent nails. There was a flimsy shelf, made out of a fence plank, loaded with tins of furniture polish and shoe blacking.

Maddie and Keith stood in silence for a while, their eyes growing accustomed to the half-light of the cupboard. Maddie wrinkled her nose. The air was heavy with the smell of polish and old dusters. Still, at least they were away from prying strangers, or so Maddie hoped.

"OK," Keith whispered, miserably. His eyes were wide, straining to see in the gloom. The strip of light from the door lay like a scar across his face. "He made me wait outside the shops. He was ages. It started to rain." Keith's teeth began to chatter, as if he were chilled by the memory.

Maddie took hold of his hands. They were icy cold.

"Poor Keith!" she said. "First he nicks your bed, then he freezes you half to death!"

Quentin had indeed taken over Keith's room. Keith now slept on a mattress out on the landing. He had refused to take it downstairs to the front room, as Mrs Palmer had suggested, because of the noises from under the floor.

"Tell it from the beginning," said Maddie. "Start with the zoo."

"We didn't go," Keith said.

"What!" said Maddie. She stared at Keith through the darkness.

He blinked and shivered and sat down abruptly, squatting on his haunches on the bare and dusty floorboards, hugging his knees to his chest. Maddie lowered herself carefully down, and knelt beside him.

"Now, Keith," she said, as she settled into a more comfortable position, "tell all!"

So Keith told all. In his earnest and faltering tones, he explained how Quentin had tried to get into the zoo, waving his tickets at the woman in the kiosk and attempting to push his way through the turnstile with Keith trailing at his heels.

"We couldn't get in, though," Keith said. "There must have been something wrong with the turnstile. It stopped turning round. The woman took our tickets away. She said they had the wrong date on them or something. Then there was a lot of shouting and some men in caps turned up and Quentin made me run all the way across the park. We hid in the bushes for a while."

Keith shivered at the memory. Then he carried on with his careful telling of the day's events. Maddie was able to picture it all quite easily. She knew her brother. She could imagine exactly how he would have behaved with Quentin; nervous and quiet, uncomplaining and polite with just the occasional display of the stubborn side of his nature.

After failing to gain entry to the zoo, something that Keith, who was afraid of most animals, whether they were in cages or not, was actually quite pleased about, Quentin, too, had seemed relieved.

"Ah well, it would have had to have been a flying visit at any rate," he said. "I am a busy man, Keith, my boy. You will be a good lad while I attend to a few chores in town, will you not? Splendid! And, of course, you'll tell your mother that you had a marvellous time, won't you? No need to mention the . . . misunderstanding at the zoo. She's a delicate flower, your mother. We wouldn't want to upset her, now would we? Jolly good!"

Quentin then made some harsh observations about the ticket woman at the zoo as they hurried across the park.

"She should consider herself lucky I did not insist upon seeing the manager! The silly old bat had obviously printed the wrong date on the tickets when I bought them and then had the nerve to start flinging all sorts of outrageous accusations at me to cover her back!"

When they passed a couple with a little girl heading in the direction from which they had come, the child skipping along, babbling excitedly about visiting the zoo, Quentin had stood in front of them and held up a hand like a traffic policeman.

"Do not, I beg you, go to that palace of infamy, the Pridebridge Zoo! Why, my boy, here, and I have just been refused entry for no reason whatsoever! The poor little lad is inconsolable!"

The toddler fell silent and rushed to hide behind her mother's legs while her parents gawped at Quentin in astonishment. He strode on, flashing them a brilliant white smile as he went, while Keith, cringing with embarrassment, hurried after him.

Once out of the park, Quentin led Keith through a warren of litter-strewn back alleys and narrow passageways that ran between closed-down works buildings and dilapidated warehouses. They eventually arrived at a mean-looking high street in a part of town that Keith had never visited before.

For Keith, this was where the waiting began.

"He went in a shop with horses painted on the window," said Keith. "The sign said it was a book shop, I think. He was in there for ages, but he can't have found any books he liked. He wasn't in a very good mood when he came out."

Quentin had bought Keith an iced bun in a baker's shop before telling him to wait on the pavement. Having been too nervous to eat breakfast, Keith was, by now, hungry enough to forget about the dead wasps he had noticed scattered along the front of the baker's window, where the cakes sat in stodgy rows. However, a ragged pigeon, with all its toes missing, hobbled over to where he was waiting and stared at him with such an accusing look in its eye that, overcome with guilt, he had thrown his bun, uneaten, to the ground. The pigeon had taken a couple of pecks then turned its back with a contemptuous squawk.

Next, Quentin visited a small and dingy shop with bars on all the windows. The shop sign bore a name, that Keith took no notice of, and a design comprising of three yellow circles or balls, arranged in a triangular pattern.

Through the bars, Keith could see tarnished rings and thick necklaces of dull gold. Inside the shop, Quentin was deep in a long conversation with a surly-looking old woman behind the counter.

Finally, Quentin emerged, again without appearing

to have bought anything, and announced that he was "Just popping into The Spread Eagle for five minutes to wet the old whistle!" Again, Keith was instructed to wait outside. He stood, watching the swinging double doors and reading the sign: OVER 21s ONLY.

After what seemed like hours Quentin had emerged briefly.

"I shan't be long," he said to Keith, "here, have an egg and diddley-dum."

He handed Keith an opened bag of ready salted crisps with a pickled egg sliding heavily around inside the packet.

At last, with the setting sun staining the clouds a vivid orange, Quentin appeared through the swinging doors of the pub, a slight smile on his face and a glazed look in his eye.

In the darkness of the understairs cupboard, Keith fell silent. Maddie let out a long breath.

"Well," she said, "that's all food for thought, make no mistake, Keith. But what I was really hoping to find out was some kind of link between Quentin and the noises under the floor. The way he acted last night when he heard that scratching sound . . . Well, it's got to mean something, hasn't it? He went absolutely mad!"

"I saw something this morning," said Keith quietly. Something in his voice made Maddie catch her breath. She waited. At last Keith spoke.

"It was an eye," he said. "An eye under the floor."

9

"An eye under the floor? Keith, are you mad? How did it get there?" Maddie had seized her brother by the hands again and was shaking him vigorously. She stopped abruptly, as it occurred to her that having your head jolted back and forth in a darkened cupboard were not the easiest conditions in which to speak.

"It was just *there*," Keith said, after getting his breath back. "Last night, remember, I was playing the marble game? You were watching TV."

"That quiz show? The questions were so easy! Carry on," said Maddie.

"Well, one of my marbles rolled down the stairs. I was looking for it this morning in the hall, up by the front door. I thought it must have got down between the wall and the side of the carpet. I looked there. I had to pull the carpet up a bit. It was like where you put the biscuit down for the mice. There was a big crack between the boards. Something was shining, down under the floor. I thought it was my marble, that it had slipped down a bit and stuck between the floorboards. Then it blinked."

"It blinked!" repeated Maddie in a stupefied whisper. "What did you do then?"

"I put the carpet back and went away," said Keith, miserably.

"What! But you didn't even tell me about it!" Maddie was often exasperated by her brother's reluctance to communicate. Why did she always have to remind him to tell her *everything*?

"I didn't want to have to show you where it was," he said, reluctantly. "I don't want to look at it again. I don't even want to walk on that bit of floor any more. I have to jump over it to get in and out of the front door."

"Right," said Maddie grimly. She placed one large palm against the door and pushed it open. Then she clambered out, still on her knees, crawling on to the floral patterned hall carpet, blinking in the electric light.

Cautiously, she peered into the kitchen. She did not want Quentin to know she had any interest in the noises under the floorboards. Maddie had an instinctive mistrust of this man who had appeared from nowhere, calling himself her father.

There was no need to worry, however.

In the kitchen, Mrs Palmer stood at the sink, washing a huge bowl full of dusty cabbage leaves.

". . . Well, and then o' course," she was saying, "mmn, yes . . . I can't abide that bitty bread. The bread with the bits in. Those bits get all in my teeth . . ."

Quentin was sitting at the table, slumped in his chair, his eyes closed and his chest rising and falling gently, a look of perfect peace on his sleeping face. Mrs Palmer's voice droned soothingly in the background.

"Right," Maddie said again and she silently heaved herself up on to her feet and tiptoed down the hall to the front door. She hooked back the carpet with her toe, maintaining her balance by spreading her arms out in a graceful arc above her head. There was nothing awkward or cumbersome about Maddie's large size. Often she displayed a delicate grace in the way she moved. Lowering herself to her knees once more, Maddie stared at the floorboards.

Something moved. Maddie held her breath for an instant then let it out in a long hiss. It was just a silverfish. Maddie pulled a face. She did not like silverfish. To her eye there was something maggot-like about them. It squirmed down into the darkness of the thin crack between the boards.

Then she saw the marble. It was made of deep blue glass, its surface patterned with cracks. A tiny image of the hall light, with its fringed shade, could be seen in glinting reflection on the rim of the tiny sphere.

Maddie returned to the cupboard under the stairs.

"You don't have to stay in there, you know Keith," she said, opening the door. "By the way, here's your phantom eyeball." She dropped the marble into Keith's open palm.

Keith stared at it.

"Still. I'm not giving up," Maddie said. "I know there's *something* down there."

"It was an *eye*," muttered Keith, "an eye, not a marble!" He trailed after Maddie, into the front room.

10

Quentin did not stay for dinner. For Maddie, this was a great relief. She had yet to exchange more than a couple of words with her newly returned father and she hoped to keep it that way for as long as possible.

The dinner had taken Mrs Palmer hours to prepare. The draining board was still buried under a heap of coiled, mud-caked potato peelings. Huge iron pots had bubbled away for hours. Two frying pans had been required to accommodate the vast amount of sausages Mrs Palmer had felt it necessary to provide for her newfound husband. Just as the meal neared completion, Quentin had woken up, stretched his arms languorously above his head and stood up.

"Much as I'd love to stay and sample some more of your delectable cookery, my dear," he said, "I must, alas, away. I have to meet a man. It's a business matter, you understand." He waved his hands airily, turned his whitest smile on Mrs Palmer and then left.

"Well! He might have waited half an hour! After you

spending so long on the dinner and all!" Maddie said hotly.

"Now don't you . . . mmm, yes . . . criticise your father!" Mrs Palmer had returned sharply. "You heard him. He's got business to attend to! Now eat your food."

Maddie stared at her plate. It was filled to the edges with a mountain of mashed potato. A pool of baked beans lay steaming in the dips and craters that covered the mound of mash. Sausages, cooked to a sooty brown, jutted out like the stumps of trees in a devastated landscape. A slippery heap of wet cabbage ran alongside the potato. Looking at her plate, Maddie recalled a documentary she had seen on the television about the First World War.

Keith jumped backwards in his chair as his mother slammed a hefty plate of bangers and mash on to the table in front of him. He stared at the brimming plateful like a small rodent caught in the gaze of a snake.

Maddie shook her head. She thought about how Quentin was treating both her mother and her brother. Then she recalled the look in Quentin's eyes on the few occasions she had been face to face with him. What did that expression mean? She shrugged, putting the question to one side for the moment, and turned her attention to the gargantuan meal before her. With a look of grim determination in her eye, she lifted her fork and began to dig in.

The air in the front room felt faintly chill. No one went in there very often. The television set in the corner remained cold and silent.

Maddie did not watch much television any more. She had watched a great deal in her younger days. She had sat alone in her wicker chair for hours on end, with the lurid colours of the small screen flickering across her enraptured features, while Mrs Palmer took Keith to and fro to nursery and later on to school, or busied herself over some household chore, calling from the kitchen, "Maddie, you'll get square eyes! Don't say I didn't warn you, mmn, yes!"

Maddie watched all the schools programmes and never forgot anything she saw. But after a while she began to lose patience with the television. The limitations of the programmes she was watching started to annoy her. She was now twelve years old, the wicker chair was upstairs in her bedroom and her patience with TV was reaching its limit.

"Turn the fire on, Keith," Maddie said, curling her feet under her legs. She was sitting on the settee. The wild daisy pattern on the cushion covers swirled away beneath and around her. Smoothing down the plain blue material of her dress, she turned half an eye on the television, yammering away in the corner by the window. She had switched it on out of habit.

Keith crawled out from under the dark stained dining table that stood against the far wall of the room. The table had long been his favourite hiding place. He was beginning to be a little too big for it. Mrs Palmer kept a clean white tablecloth spread over the tabletop and a vase filled with faded artificial flowers as a centrepiece. Their frayed stems and curling petals were coated with a thick layer of dust. No meals were ever taken in the front room.

Keith hunched over the old gas fire with a box of matches. Maddie aired her thoughts aloud. At the same time, she answered the questions that were being asked by a cheery voiced TV quiz show presenter.

"OK Keith," she said. "Here's the plan. Capital of Mexico? Mexico City. Huh! How laughably easy! Tonight, I'm going to wait until it's way past midnight, until I'm sure everyone is asleep, particularly a certain very suspicious acting father I could mention, and then . . . Battle of Agincourt! Battle of Agincourt, you moron! . . . then I'm going to creep downstairs to check out our biscuit under the floorboards. I'm sure I can prise that board loose without making too much noise and reach down to get it. Whatever it is down there, and don't forget this father of ours nearly had a fit when he heard it scratching about, it's bound to have at least nibbled at the biscuit and that'll give me a clue as to what on earth it is. Robert Louis Stevenson, you dunderhead! Hurry up with that fire, Keith, I'm freezing!"

The batteries were running low on Maddie's torch. She cursed herself, silently, for not having checked earlier in the day. The pool of sickly yellow light was growing dimmer by the minute and she had not yet got the nails out of the floorboard. It was proving far harder than she had imagined.

Suddenly, Maddie froze. There was the shuffle of a footstep on the stair. Slowly, she reached out and cupped her hand around the torch. All was dark now, but for a wafer-thin streak of light, a red glow between Maddie's fingers. The soft, hesitant footstep descended the stair. A light tread, like the sprinkle of rain on a window. Maddie breathed a sigh of relief. She stood up, lifting her torch and letting its dying light spill over her face. She held a finger to her lips and glared up at the banisters.

Keith was about halfway down the stairs. He gave a gasp as he saw his sister, her face illuminated from below, her features picked out in an eerie orange glow.

"Keith!" Maddie mouthed. "Come down here!"

Keith pattered down the stairs. Dressed in rumpled pyjamas, several sizes too small for him, the trousers halfway up his skinny shins, he stood shivering in the near darkness.

"What are you doing, Keith? For goodness' sake, you'll catch a cold!" Maddie scolded him in a low whisper.

"I thought you might need this," Keith said. He held up his own small pocket torch and carefully clicked on the switch. A strong beam lit up the hallway.

Maddie looked at her brother, holding out the torch to her with an uncertain look on his face. She knew he did not like the dark. And she knew how much whatever he had seen down under the floor had scared him. She had not asked him to join her on this late night expedition. And yet here he was, past midnight, shivering in the downstairs hallway.

"You're braver than you look, Keith Palmer," she whispered, laying her large hand gently on his bony shoulder. "Whatever would I do without you?"

Maddie took Keith's torch and knelt down by the kitchen door. She had pulled the carpet right back, exposing an expanse of bare boards still covered by a heavy sprinkling of black dust. The handle of a screwdriver jutted out from the crack between the wooden boards, which Maddie had been using to painstakingly prise the nails loose before hooking them out with a claw hammer. Laying the torch on the ground, she got back to working on the nails while Keith stood and watched, shifting from foot to foot and glancing nervously up at the staircase every now and again.

At last, the final nail came groaning out of the wooden joist. Maddie lifted up the floorboard and laid it carefully on the carpet behind her. Keith backed away a little to give her room.

There was a deep silence in the house, broken only by the sound of Maddie's breathing and the occasional trickle as fragments of crumbled underlay slipped into the dark abyss. She reached out and lifted the torch, shining it into the space beneath the floorboards. Floating motes of dust glowed like flakes of gold, hanging suspended against a backdrop of velvet darkness. Maddie leant forward and peered into the hole.

Beneath the floor there was a space of about half a metre. Then there was the ground. Picked out in a circle of torchlight, Maddie could see nothing but dry, grey dirt and powdery white dust. She shifted the torch beam this way and that.

Then she saw the biscuit. It lay amidst a pile of crushed rubble, apparently untouched, the string coiled around it like the tail of a sleeping dormouse.

Maddie shifted her knees on the folded back carpet and leant a bit further forward. She reached down, one handed, feeling the cold air flowing around her wrist and sweating palm. Her fingers closed on the familiar round edge of the chocolate chip cookie.

Suddenly a wave of fear washed over her. Some change, some subtle movement, perhaps no more than the lifting of an eyelid, had altered the atmosphere beneath the floor. She felt as if she were being watched, not by Keith, but by someone else. Someone under the floor.

In a wild panic, Maddie yanked her hand back. In the same instant, she heard a shuffling scramble beneath her. She could not restrain a bellow of terror as she felt something try to grab hold of her wrist.

She threw herself backwards, knocking the torch flying. It dropped into the gap in the floor and everything was plunged into darkness.

11

After a heart-stopping few seconds of blind panic the hall light snapped on and Maddie struggled to her knees, blinking in the unaccustomed glare. Heavy footsteps pounded down the stairs.

In a daze, Maddie turned her head and looked up. Quentin towered above her. He was wearing a red dressing gown made of a silky looking material. He glared down at her. His oiled hair was uncombed and jutted out at all angles.

"What are you doing?" he snapped, his lips curled back from his white, white teeth in a snarl of rage. He was angry, that was plain. But he also looked afraid.

Maddie could not take in what he was saying. She was not able to listen. Something had touched her. Something moving. Something alive. A hand had grabbed at her. Long fingers had tried to grasp her by the wrist. Then something large had slithered away beneath the floor. The thought of it filled her mind.

"What are you doing?" Quentin repeated. He

struggled to control his voice and managed to restore a little of the bell-like quality to his tone. Raising his arm jerkily, he smoothed down his hair with the palm of one hand.

"Would you kindly explain to me, Madeline," he said, "what you are doing down here, in the middle of the night, with half the floorboards ripped up?"

"Just one floorboard, actually," Maddie muttered, "and no one ever calls me Madeline."

They glared at each other for a second. Then Quentin let out a little snorting breath and turned to Keith, who was standing, eyes wide and skin as white as chalk, by the front-room door.

"And you can leave my brother alone too," Maddie snapped, "he'll not tell you anything."

"I see," said Quentin. The ghost of a smile seemed to play about his lips. "Well, you are children, after all. And children must have their games, mustn't they?" He took a deep breath then flashed his startling smile. "But I want you both to promise me that you won't go poking around under the floor again. From the noises I've heard coming from down there I suspect we have an infestation. What we have," and Quentin raised his voice, "is a problem with vermin! But don't worry," he boomed, "I'll be taking care of things. Vermin," and now he was shouting again, "can be STAMPED OUT!" Quentin brought his heel down hard on the floral patterned hall carpet with a reverberating thud.

Mrs Palmer appeared at the top of the stairs wearing a limp yellow nightdress.

"Is that Maddie again, having one of her . . . mmn, yes . . . midnight feasts?" she said. Ignoring her, Quentin placed one hand on Maddie's shoulder, the other on Keith's.

"I hope I've made myself clear," he said, his voice tolling like a warning bell. "I will deal with our problem below the floorboards. Now, to bed with you!"

Quentin smiled again, his teeth gleaming white in the hallway's electric light. His eyes, however, remained cold.

Quentin rose early the next morning. Maddie, lying in bed, heard him yawn and cough. He was still sleeping in Keith's room. She heard his knees click as he stood up and his bare feet on the carpet as he strode across the landing. Even without his shiny black shoes on, his step still seemed full of boundless self-confidence. Maddie noted the extra big stride as Quentin stepped over Keith, who was lying on the landing in his sleeping bag. She listened as Quentin brushed his teeth noisily, spitting with great gusto and humming to himself with apparent contentment. It seemed to Maddie, lying in the darkness of her room, that he was aware of listening ears and that his every move was part of some elaborate performance.

After listening to Quentin make his way downstairs, stumbling once and biting back a curse as he accidentally kicked something large down the steps, Maddie got out of bed. She crossed to the window and drew back the curtain. There was no sign of dawn in the purple night sky. The streetlamp opposite the house filled the room with a dingy light.

Maddie blinked in the dull half-light. Something had moved, down in the street. She opened her eyes wide. A manhole cover in the middle of the road shifted slightly. Maddie stared. Had she imagined it? No, it moved again. There was the faint scrape of metal over asphalt as the circular iron cover was pushed aside. A man climbed out of the hole in the road.

Tall and thin, he stood beside the open manhole with his back to the house. The dark coloured overalls he wore hung loosely from his bony frame. His shaven head turned this way and that, glancing all around. He appeared cautious but unhurried. Casually, he pushed the manhole cover back into place using his feet and he somehow managed to make very little noise as he did so. The streetlamp turned his pale skin a glistening orange.

The man stiffened, as if he had suddenly sensed that someone was watching him. Slowly, he began to turn around. Maddie found her curiosity suddenly give way to instinctive alarm. She did not know who this man was. She supposed he was probably a sewer worker who had just finished a night shift. Nevertheless she realised that she had no wish to see his face or to look into his eyes. And she certainly did not want him to see her, standing at her darkened window staring out into the street. She slipped back out of sight and sank to the floor, her back against the wall and her heart pounding in her chest.

12

Maddie lay on her bed a while. The tarnished silver light of a cloudy November dawn slowly seeped into the room. She looked at the ceiling. Now that it was lighter, she could make out the various tiny cracks in the plaster. They were comfortingly familiar.

The ceiling was like the map of a mighty river and its tributaries, snaking through a bleak snow-scape. Only the occasional forest of trailing spider's web, or a frozen lake where a patch of paint had flaked off, broke the monotony of the endless barren wastes. Maddie estimated the length, in centimetres, of the longest of the plaster-crack rivers. She needed to calm her nerves.

Why had the unexpected appearance of the sewer worker given her such a fright? Last night, something had grabbed at her hand in the dark below the floorboards. And yet seeing this man clambering out of a hole in the road was somehow just as chilling. Maddie puzzled it over. There had been something in his movements, she realised, something in the slope of his shoulders, the shape of his head that had seemed uncomfortably familiar. But, try as she might, Maddie could not place it. The familiarity was too faint, even for Maddie's phenomenal memory, to make any connections. Perhaps, she thought, she was still feeling the effects of the alarming experience of the night before. She put it to the back of her mind and turned her thoughts to her father.

The sewer man was not Quentin, of that, at least, she was sure. She had been listening to his sonorous humming floating up from downstairs for over an hour. A range of other sounds accompanied the bursts of wordless song. Sawing, the squeal of nails extracted from wood, the clump of heavy tools and the occasional violent curse rang out in the still of the morning.

Maddie waited. She did not want Quentin to suspect that he was being observed. She would go down at breakfast time, as usual, and eat in the kitchen. With any luck she would be able to see what the man was up to, without appearing to be taking any notice.

At eight o'clock, Maddie pulled on the blue dress that she had left draped over the foot of her bed the night before, and went out on to the landing. Mrs Palmer was hovering by the bathroom, a great pile of dirty laundry in her arms. Keith was sitting up, his sleeping bag pulled up to his neck, silently staring into space. Maddie stepped over her brother and peered down the stairs.

"Don't disturb your father . . . mmm, yes . . ." Mrs Palmer said, in a conspiratorial whisper, "he's doing a bit of DIY."

Maddie gave her mother a hard look.

"I'm going to have breakfast," she said coldly. She headed quickly downstairs. At the bottom step, she stopped.

Quentin was in the hall. The floorboards by the kitchen had all been taken up. There was a large, straight-sided hole in the floor. Quentin was squatting at the foot of the stairs staring at the hole like a cat looking into a fishpond. He glanced up at Maddie.

"A very good morning to you!" he said.

Maddie sniffed and made a vague word-like sound under her breath.

"If you want to get into the kitchen you'll have to step on the crossbeams." Quentin indicated the hole in the floor. Some lengths of thick wood, laid across low squares of brick, spanned the area by the kitchen door. These beams are what the floorboards had been nailed to. They were grey with the dust of ages.

Seeing Maddie make no move to go back upstairs, Quentin stood up, giving her room to pass. Without a moment's hesitation, she walked along the narrow beam, placing one foot delicately in front of the other, and into the kitchen. She let the kitchen door swing open and walked over to the fridge without turning round.

"You're not a girl that's easily put off, are you, Maddie?" Quentin's tones sounded unusually sincere, as if he was thinking aloud rather than putting on his usual vocal extravaganza for the benefit of all listeners.

Maddie poured herself a glass of milk, stooped down and pulled a loaf of sliced bread in its plastic packaging out of a large cardboard box by the back door. As she prepared breakfast, she mulled over what she had seen of the area beneath the floorboards. Something had definitely disturbed the ground. But the marks in the dusty earth were too regular and too straight to have been caused by rats or mice. What she had seen, Maddie was convinced, were scrapings in the soil made with some kind of tool. A small trowel, perhaps.

Maddie pulled out the grill pan, thrust her hand into the bread bag and began laying the white slices out on the grill. Behind her she could hear Quentin humming again. She chanced a quick look over her shoulder. He was lashing a length of thick cord around a section of the banisters. Quentin looked up and grinned at her. It was as if he had known Maddie would be watching. Now he tied the other end of the cord around his waist.

Maddie looked out into the garden through the window in the back door. The washing line could usually be seen, shifting in the wind, with a few dozen wooden clothes pegs clipped on to it at irregular intervals. It was missing.

She turned back to Quentin. He was crouched at the edge of the hole in the floor. Keith's torch was tucked into his belt. He smiled at Maddie once again and raised his hand in a jaunty salute.

"No sense in taking any chances," he said, pulling at the knotted cord to test its strength. "Pull me up if you hear screams, there's a good girl." With that he jumped down into the hole and then disappeared, head first, under the floorboards.

Maddie turned back to the grill and flipped the

toast over, one slice at a time. She was now convinced that someone had been crawling around under the house. Whoever it was, it had been their hand that had tried to grab her the previous night. It had been their eye that Keith had seen, glittering in the darkness beneath the boards. Maddie knew it, and so, she was sure, did Quentin.

13

Later, back in her room, Maddie lay on the bed again. The springs clicked and clanged as she shifted into a more comfortable position. Downstairs, Quentin was working frantically. She could hear him moving around, breathing hard, dragging something heavy across the hall carpet. Mrs Palmer was out, taking Keith to school. The front door was wide open. The house was filled with the dank atmosphere of the world outside.

Maddie had retreated to her room and closed the door. Even so, she could not completely escape the feeling of panic that the open door had stirred inside her. It was like being on the deck of a ship, knowing that there was an enormous hole beneath the waterline and that gallons of seawater were flooding in. And yet she also knew she was in no real danger. It was a nameless, buried fear, something she had not yet been able to bring into the light. It forced her to live in terror of the outside world and kept her a prisoner in her own home.

She tried clearing her mind by staring at the rose pattern wallpaper, following, with her eyes, the complex pathways of intertwined tendrils and the rows of curling petals. Then she took a deep breath and turned her mind to Quentin and what he was doing downstairs.

Maddie clambered off the bed and crossed to the window. She had just heard him go out into the front garden. Looking down, she saw him, shirtsleeves rolled up, his oiled hair a tousled mess, knees bent and with the veins standing out in his arms as he struggled to prise up one of the flagstones from the path with his bare hands. After five minutes of grunting exertion, he managed to lift the flagstone and drag it into the house. Maddie heard the dull thump as the heavy stone crossed the front step. Then there was a muffled scraping sound as Quentin hauled it over the carpet to the hole in the floor.

Maddie sat down in her wicker chair and let its familiar creaking and crackling surround her. The normal pattern of life in the Palmer household was being rapidly dismantled. Quentin was digging up the front path, dragging the flagstones through the house and depositing them underneath the floorboards. And worse still, he had left the front door wide open while he did it.

It was clear that Quentin had found something under the floor and that it had galvanised him into his current frenzy of activity. Maddie wondered what her mother would say when she found the front path was missing. Mrs Palmer, however, seemed to have decided not to return to the house straight away. She was probably putting in an extra visit to Saver's Paradise or had gone to Cheapo-Mart to compare the prices. In any case, Maddie suspected that her mother would find nothing amiss in Quentin's behaviour. She would see it as another part of the mysterious world of men, the rules of which she had neither the desire nor the ability to question.

Maddie shifted in her wicker chair. The wicker creaked and crackled in protest. Outside in the street Quentin had disappeared into the front garden of the house next door. Mr and Mrs Shale lived there.

To Maddie, the Shales were shadowy figures. An anonymous-looking middle-aged couple with no children, they both worked long hours and were seldom at home. Maddie recalled how once, whilst watching a house sparrow that had nested in the gutter of the building opposite teach its young to fly, she had looked down and noticed Mr Shale, the top of his balding head reddening in the sunshine as he irritably rebuilt his front garden wall on last August Bank Holiday. Occasionally Maddie would glance out of her bedroom window and see one or the other of them coming in or going out. Other than that, they were invisible.

Now Quentin confidently stepped over the Shale's brick wall and bent down, out of the range of Maddie's vision. When he straightened, she saw that he was carrying in his arms an unopened but very grubby-looking polythene sack with the words READY-MIX CEMENT & SAND printed on it in faded orange letters. It must have been left over from Mr Shale's wall building. Now Quentin had stolen it.

The bag must have been heavy. Quentin was carrying it with both hands. He did not climb back over the wall. Instead he left via the gate.

But his exertions seemed to be getting the better of him. As he headed back along the pavement he stumbled under the weight of the bag of cement mix and, in trying to right himself, went staggering off the kerb and into the gutter. He managed to stop himself falling over. Taking a firmer grip on the bag, Quentin turned and was about to step back up on to the kerb.

Maddie gave a gasp of horror. There was a drain in the road down by Quentin's feet. The heavy iron drain cover had been pushed aside. A long-fingered hand shot out and seized him by the ankle. Quentin let out a strangled cry of surprise and alarm. The cement bag fell to the ground.

Up at the window, Maddie covered her eyes.

14

When Maddie looked again Quentin was standing at the garden gate, bent double, breathing hard. After a minute or two, he crept back out to the pavement, moving cautiously. Keeping his feet as far away from the open drain as possible, he stretched out his hand and seized a corner of the cement bag. With a sudden burst of speed, he dragged the cement over the kerb and up what had once been the garden path. Maddie stared. Had she really seen a hand rise up from the open drain?

Maddie could hear Quentin clattering around downstairs, running the taps in the kitchen, slopping water around, stamping about in the hallway, grunting and panting from exertion. And then she heard, with great relief, the front door swing shut. She stood up. Now that the door to the outside was closed, she felt she could face anything.

"Right then," she said aloud, "let's see what's going on, shall we?"

Maddie was on the last stair before Quentin noticed

her. He was crouched by the hole in the hall floor, mixing wet cement in the washing-up bowl, briskly stirring the thick grey mixture with a fish slice. His white shirt was torn and filthy, his hair a wilderness of jutting clumps. He was muttering to himself under his breath.

But despite his obvious distraction, Quentin was still able to put on his usual relaxed manner and resonant, bell-like voice as soon as he became aware that Maddie was behind him.

"Ah, Madeline!" he said, without turning around. "I was wondering when curiosity would get the better of you. I'm sure you're very curious about what I've been doing. Well, I'll tell you about it. I've been doing you all a favour, as a matter of fact. I've been filling in a rather large hole that I found, way down under your floorboards, back that way," and he inclined his head, indicating the direction of the front door. "I used a few spare flagstones that I found lying about the place. And now I'm going to cement them into place just to make sure nothing can get through. Something's been getting in, as you know. Noises under the floor and all that. But not any more. Father's dealt with it, just as he said he would. You can forget all about it now."

At this point Quentin turned around. Despite the melodic chiming of his voice, there was a wild look, somewhere deep in his eye. He fixed Maddie with an unblinking stare. There was a tense silence.

"I am reminded," he said at last, "of a certain famous expression. About what curiosity did to the cat? I'm sure it was a situation such as this which led to the demise of the cat in question.

"A cat owner, perhaps indulging in a spot of DIY, takes up the floorboards for an hour or two, then hammers them down again, little knowing that his cat has slipped down under the floor and is now sealed up below the boards. At first the cat is happy enough. There are plenty of mice and rats to chase. Being a little deaf, the cat owner hears nothing. Still, he begins to wonder what has become of his cat. As the days pass he becomes increasingly convinced that Pusskins has met his end out on the nearby motorway. The cat, meanwhile, has devoured every living creature under the floor and is eager to return to the world above. He yowls and mews in increasingly despairing tones. The man, mourning the death of his cat, says to himself, 'You know, I could almost swear I can hear old Pusskin's meowing sometimes. Funny how the mind plays tricks!'

Gradually the meowing gets fainter and fainter, then stops altogether. The ex-cat owner buys himself a budgerigar."

"That's a horrid story," said Maddie after a short pause.

"It's a horrid world," said Quentin softly, "or, at least . . . it can be."

And then, as if realising that he had strayed too far out of character, Quentin bared his gleaming white teeth in a hearty smile.

"What happened outside?" Maddie said, ignoring the smile. "I saw someone grab you. Someone down in the drain, they reached up and . . ."

"Hah!" Quentin let out a bark of laughter. "Very good, Madeline, very good indeed!" he said. "I tripped on the drain cover. It seems to have been knocked out of kilter. Perhaps a passing car or lorry . . .? I really should inform the local council. There was a twig or something, the rain had half washed it away. It was jutting out of the drain. And what was it you say you saw, from your first floor window? A monstrous hand coming up from the underworld?"

"I didn't say it was monstrous," Maddie said, quietly but firmly. "It was a hand, a man's hand."

"Oh, it's a wonderful thing, Maddie," smiled Quentin, "the imagination of a child!"

Maddie did not smile back.

15

"Why can't he sleep with Mum? I mean, that's what married people are supposed to do, isn't it?"

"Keith! Don't be disgusting!"

"Well, I'm fed up with sleeping out on the landing!" Keith muttered. He folded his arms and knitted his brows. Maddie looked at him, surprised. Compared to his usual passive behaviour, this seemed like out and out rebellion.

"Steady on, Keith," she said, "you'll be chewing the carpet next!"

"I *am* fed up, though!"

"Yes, yes. I know. It must be rotten. Everyone stepping over you on their way to the bathroom in the mornings."

"Stepping over and, sometimes, *on* me," Keith said pointedly.

"Oh, yes, sorry about that," Maddie said, "I'm not always at my best before breakfast time."

The two children were sitting on Maddie's bed in the

fading light of the late afternoon. The weather was overcast. A gust of wind, like a discontented sigh, breathed on the windows, causing them to rattle in their frames. A few raindrops spattered against the glass.

"Shall I turn on the light?" Keith said. Daylight was draining rapidly from the sky. Maddie's bedroom was deep in shadow.

She grunted her assent.

"The streetlight's just come on," she said, idly. "I'd love to be watching at the exact moment it switches on. I must try and do that one day . . ."

There was a pause. A fresh smattering of raindrops peppered the window.

"He still hasn't left the house," Maddie said, "and he's definitely looking for something."

She was talking about Quentin. She and Keith had spoken of little else since his arrival. Maddie felt the need to run through everything Quentin did, aloud, as a way of clarifying her thoughts. She was determined to figure out what it was Quentin was up to. Keith was a good listener. He was also the only person Maddie had to talk to.

She had contemplated confronting Quentin head-on. But something in his manner urged her to caution.

The look in his eye as he sat at the edge of the hole in the floor lingered in Maddie's mind.

She had tried talking to her mother. She had made an attempt that morning.

"Mum," Maddie had said, finding her in the kitchen, washing up, while Quentin prowled around the front room, kicking the skirting boards and tapping the walls with his knuckles, "he's acting a bit weird, isn't he? Don't you think there's something, you know, *odd* about him?"

"If it's your father you're talking about," Mrs Palmer said, looking up sharply, "then I think you've got a cheek, Maddie girl, to question your elders and betters!"

"But Mum . . ."

"Not another, mmm yes, word! He may have strange habits, but he's still your father!" Mrs Palmer glared at her daughter, head tipped to one side, her thin lips pursed in anger. Maddie turned on her heel and stalked away, stamping upstairs to her room with the sound of Quentin, still tapping at the walls, echoing in the hallway.

Now, as the winter evening closed in, Maddie was still in her room. Keith had joined her after getting back from school. Quentin, having spent hours in the front room, seemingly examining every inch of floor, wall, ceiling and anything in-between, had moved on to the kitchen and was now rooting around in the cupboard under the stairs.

"He said he's making an invention," said Keith miserably. "I don't want him to make an invention. What will it do?"

"What are you talking about, Keith?"

"It's what he said. He called out as I went past the cupboard under the stairs. He said he was making an invention of the whole house."

"An *inventory*, twit! He must have said inventory. It's like a list of everything in the house. So that's what he's pretending to be up to, is it? Pah! I don't believe him. He's looking for something."

"But how do you know, Maddie?" Keith said quietly.

"Oh, I know all right," said Maddie. "D'you remember that really old Tarzan film that we watched on the telly once?"

"The black and white one, with the rubber crocodiles?"

Both Maddie and her brother had powerful memories. They were able to discuss television programmes they had seen years ago.

"Yes, that's the one," Maddie continued. "Well, d'you remember the bit where the hunters started killing all the animals? Tarzan knew, didn't he, even though he was on totally the opposite side of the jungle? He could sense something was wrong in his world. Well, that's what I'm like. This house is my world, and there's something wrong. Quentin's a hunter, make no mistake. The question is; what is he hunting? And what are you smirking at, all of a sudden, Keith?" Maddie had noticed a broad grin spread across her brother's face while she was speaking.

"You," said Keith, "and Tarzan." He shivered with silent mirth for a moment or two, doubtless imagining his sister swinging through the jungle canopy on specially strengthened vine ropes, dressed in a leopard skin swimsuit.

"Well, at least that's cheered you up a bit," said Maddie. "But the problem still remains. How do I find out what Quentin's up to? And who was the man in the drain? Could it be the same person, making the noises under the hall? It could have been him all along, coming in through the sewers and crawling about under our floorboards," – Keith shivered at this and slapped a hand over his mouth, as if to stifle a cry of fear. "But what's the connection between him and Quentin?" Maddie went on. "I need clues, Keith, clues!"

"I think there might be one downstairs," said Keith, his eyes lighting up. "A clue, I mean. There's a piece of paper on the front-room floor. It's Quentin's. I saw him drop it. He didn't notice though, and I didn't want to say anything to him, or pick it up, so I just left it there. There's writing on it, I think."

"It could be nothing," said Maddie, "and he might have found it already, but it's still worth a look. Nice one, Keith," she said, struggling off the bed and on to her feet. "You stay here. I'll just sneak down and see if it's there. I'd better not let Quentin see me. I can't imagine he'd be too pleased with anyone he caught reading his notes, even if it's just a shopping list."

Maddie kicked off her plimsolls as she left the room. Barefoot, she moved along the landing with delicate, noiseless steps.

She took even greater care navigating the stairs. Slowly, one step at a time, she inched her way down, all the while listening to Quentin rummaging around in the cupboard just below her feet. Only a few centimetres of wood and plaster, and a metre or so of dusty air, separated them.

She reached the hallway without making a sound and glided silently into the front room. She could hear her mother washing up next door in the kitchen, humming tunelessly to herself as she did so.

Luckily, the front-room door was wide open. There was always a chance the hinges would have squeaked and given her away. She crept into the room without turning on the light and knelt down. It was dark. She opened her eyes wide and waited for her sight to adjust to the gloom. There was something white on the floor. She stretched out her hand. A piece of paper. She picked it up and held it close to her face.

Slowly, she got to her feet and turned back to face the door.

Quentin was standing in the doorway.

16

"I thought it was Keith's. Something Keith dropped. Part of his . . . his homework, yes, his homework."

Maddie, blinking in the electric light that Quentin had just switched on, was aware that she was babbling. She was also conscious of the fact that she had never said so many words to Quentin all in one go before. He smiled his white smile.

"Homework, eh? A bit young for homework, isn't he?"

"They start young these days," Maddie said, returning Quentin's level gaze, her face like granite.

"Well, it's not Keith's. It's mine," he said, his smile gone in a trice. "Give it to me. Now!" He held out his hand.

Maddie handed over the piece of paper without looking at it. Quentin folded it into a small square and pushed it into the breast pocket of his jacket.

She hoped Quentin had not seen her scan the laboriously scrawled note just after the lights burst on.

Through a stratosphere of floating starbursts, Maddie had read Quentin's note. An image of the crumpled sheet was firmly imprinted in her mind's eye.

As she climbed back up the stairs, with Quentin watching her in silence from the front-room doorway, she recalled the words, written in biro on a grubby piece of cheap writing paper.

Small rose leaf – 234–13 S

And at the top of the sheet, there was a printed heading:

H.M. Prison: Wail Island

Maddie walked into the bedroom.

"Food for thought, Keith," she said. Keith looked up.

"Talking of which," Maddie said, "a slice or two of bread and peanut butter wouldn't go amiss."

"I'll get it," said Keith.

Maddie sat down in the wicker chair.

"Two three four, dash, one, three, 'S'." She spoke the numbers out loud. "Two hundred and thirty-four to thirteen?" she tried. Her large fingers drummed on the arm of the chair. When Keith returned with a loaf of sliced bread, a jar of peanut butter and two glasses of milk, balanced precariously on the edge of the plate, Maddie was deep in thought, her brows furrowed in concentration. He squatted on the floor next to her chair. Every once in a while he lifted the plate up and guided his sister's hand on to a slice of bread. She ate mechanically, without breaking concentration. At last she stood up, smoothed down her dress and shook her head.

"Blast!" she said, with some feeling. "I can't figure out what it means. It seems so . . . familiar somehow. I ought to know what it is!" She aimed a kick at the leg of her wicker chair.

"Oh well," Maddie pushed her hair back, tucking the loose strands behind her ears, "I'll just have to stop thinking about it for a while. It'll come to me in time."

But was time on her side, she wondered? Quentin's mood swings and peculiar behaviour were becoming increasingly worrying. If Quentin were looking for something, what would happen when he found it?

* * *

All that evening, Quentin stayed in the cupboard under the stairs, refusing to join the family for dinner. Maddie found herself obliged to eat double portions of her mother's glutinous stew with suet dumplings.

At nine forty, Maddie climbed the stairs to her bedroom. Quentin was still tapping and scratching in the understairs cupboard beneath her feet. When she woke up the next morning, Keith was standing by her bedside, staring down at her through wide eyes.

"Morning, Keith," she said, yawning and flexing her toes beneath the duvet. Keith remained silent. He gnawed at his bottom lip.

"Is something the matter?" said Maddie. Keith looked down at her. He opened his mouth to speak, then closed it again.

"I was having the most dreadful nightmare," Maddie continued, rubbing both eyes with her large fists. "Someone was trying to build a gallows. You know, one of those wooden things they used to hang people on in the old days? They were building one just outside the house. I was watching from my window. The gallows kept falling down, though, for some reason."

Maddie stopped. She had just heard a choked scream from out on the landing. Suddenly wide awake, she sat bolt upright in bed.

"Mum!" she called out. "What is it? What's happened?"

"Oh . . . mmm, yes . . .!" came Mrs Palmer's voice. "Where's it gone?"

"What's she talking about?" said Maddie, swinging her legs around and out from under the bedclothes.

"He's taken the stairs away, Maddie," Keith said, in a voice so quiet it was almost a whisper. "Quentin's taken away the stairs!"

17

They stood together on the landing. All three of them were wearing dressing gowns and had bare feet. They stared in wide-eyed silence. Then Maddie took a step forward and leant on the balustrade. She looked down. It was true. The stairs were gone.

Below her, the bare boards that last night had been the floor of the understairs cupboard, now lay exposed.

"Where is he?" Maddie said, quietly.

They all turned their eyes to the door of Keith's old room. It was closed.

"Now, Maddie," said Mrs Palmer, raising a bony finger, "I daresay your father knows what he's doing, mmn, yes. It's a spot of DIY, that's all. He's probably out at the joiners now, picking up some lovely new wood for a lovely new staircase!"

"Was there something wrong with the old one?" said Keith.

"Of course there wasn't!" Maddie said, exasperation in her voice. "He's been looking for something, I told you. And now he's made pretty sure that there's nothing hidden in the staircase!"

"What are you on about, Maddie Palmer?" her mother said in querulous tones.

Maddie sighed.

"Mum," she said. But Mrs Palmer's eyes had filled with tears.

Maddie turned away and looked over the balustrade once again. The hall carpet lay rolled up by the front door. The pots, buckets, bowls and boots, all the things that had formerly lined the stairs, had been heaped in the front room. The edge of the heap was just visible through the open doorway. Leaning against the wall between the kitchen and front-room doorway was a stack of planks, the long twisted nails still jutting out of them here and there. This timber had, until very recently, been part of the stairs. Opposite what used to be the top of the staircase, the bathroom door was wide open. Some more wooden planks had been stacked up against the wall below the towel rail.

"You're going to have to face it, Mum," Maddie said, "there's something not right about Quentin."

"Oh Maddie," Mrs Palmer gave a tearful croak, "I do wish you'd call him Father!"

"Really?" Maddie looked her mother in the eye.

There was a pause. Keith crept quietly over to the door of his old bedroom. His hand was on the doorknob. He looked at Maddie. She nodded. Keith turned the handle and the door swung open.

The bedroom was small. Shelves lined one wall. Several dozen shoeboxes and old biscuit tins, filled with worn-looking plastic figures, construction kit pieces and model cars, the paint peeling from their metal chassis, were lined up in neat rows along the shelves. Below the shelves, the narrow bed took up most of the floor space, its head below the window, its foot close to the door. On the bed, looking large and out of place in the tiny room, lay Quentin.

He was still fully dressed. The candlewick bedspread had been pulled over his shoulders. He lay with his head down at the foot of the bed, his face turned to one side, the cheek flattened against the bare mattress. His feet, clad in shiny black shoes, lay on the pillow. Deep breaths burbled out through his lips in a slow, repetitive rhythm, like waves breaking gently on a sleepy shore.

Mrs Palmer grabbed Maddie by the wrist. She pressed one bony finger against her daughter's lips.

"Shhh! We didn't ought to wake him up!" she said. "He's been working ever so hard!"

"Working hard to demolish our stairs, you mean!" Maddie said loudly.

Quentin, his sleep disturbed, snorted and smacked his lips before sinking back into slumber. Maddie glared at him.

"Wake up!" she said fiercely.

Quentin opened an eye. He gazed sightlessly up at Maddie.

"Wake up!" she said again.

Mrs Palmer slowly edged her way behind Maddie's broad back. Keith, however, took a hesitant step forward, as if to shield his sister with his tiny frame. Quentin raised his head.

"Good morning, family," he said, in a deep and sonorous tone of voice.

He suddenly swung his legs off the bed and was on his feet in an instant, wide awake and staring at Maddie with glittering eyes.

"I expect you're all wondering why I've removed the stairs," he said. "You may be wondering how you're going to get down to the kitchen or the garden or the telephone or the front door." Quentin began pacing up and down the thin strip of flooring beside Keith's bed. "I expect you, Madeline, are wondering all sorts of other things," he continued. "Things like why I took Keith on an outing with some fake zoo tickets, why I've occasionally, shall we say, lost my composure on hearing certain strange sounds from below the floor, why I filled the foundations with a solid barricade of cement and paving slabs, and why I've been searching this dreary little house, inch by inch."

Quentin smiled his white smile. Maddie, stunned into silence, could only stare at him. Keith and Mrs Palmer had frozen. All eyes were on the smiling man.

"All your questions will be answered in time," he said. "First things first, however. How are you going to get downstairs? Well, I'll tell you. You're not. You're staying right here. The time for play-acting and deception is over.

"You should consider yourselves my prisoners. Do exactly as you're told and no one will get hurt. Attempt to interfere with my plans, however, and . . . well . . . things could get nasty." Quentin smiled, but his eyes remained cold. "Things could get very nasty indeed."

18

Maddie gazed around her mother's room. She shivered. This room always chilled her to the bone. Even the sunflowers, repeated endlessly in the wallpaper pattern, seemed to be turning their faded lemon petals away from the warmth and light of the window, and were directing their cold gaze inward instead.

A framed picture was hanging, off-centre and slightly crooked, on the wall above the bed. It was a washed-out print depicting a furtive-looking robin redbreast perched on a flowerpot in a snow-covered garden.

A lumpy eiderdown covered the bed. Its silky brown fabric was cold and slippery to the touch. Maddie, Keith and Mrs Palmer were sitting on the bed. Their hands were tied behind their backs. The washing line that Quentin had taken from the garden had been used to lash them all together by the wrists.

Back to back, they sat in silence. Occasionally one of the springs in the mattress would ping as Maddie shifted herself into a marginally less uncomfortable position. A galaxy of dust motes hung in the air like fading stars, barely moving in the stale and lifeless atmosphere of the room.

"Well," said Maddie, breaking the heavy silence at last, "this is fun."

"He said he'd tell us," Keith said quietly.

"Oh, he'll tell us all right," said Maddie, her voice edged with anger, "he'll tell us what he's up to and who he really is, make no mistake. He's a showman. He's just making us wait, that's all, until he's ready to take his curtain call. Arrogant pig!"

"Now, Maddie, mmm, yes . . ." Mrs Palmer said, "don't you talk about your . . ." She hesitated.

"Yes?" said Maddie, pouncing. " 'Don't you talk about your father like that' – is that what you were going to say? Ha!"

"I was sure it was him," Mrs Palmer said. Her voice was dull and she spoke reluctantly. "But . . . now that all this has happened . . . I'm beginning to wonder . . . Mmm, yes . . . I'm afraid you didn't get your wonderful memory off me, Maddie love." Mrs Palmer's voice was choked with misery. "Even so," she went on, "now that I think about it . . . I'm sure he used to be taller!"

"Oh, Mum!" Maddie let out an exasperated sigh.

"And there's another thing . . ." Mrs Palmer was now speaking with even greater reluctance than before, "another thing I remember . . . about the picture . . . I didn't think of it till now, I swear . . ."

"Picture?" Maddie snapped. "What picture? What are you talking about, Mum?"

"The picture that used to be in the front room. On the mantelpiece. The one in the silver frame. The picture of your father." Mrs Palmer spoke slowly and reluctantly.

"What about it?" Maddie said.

"It's been there so long I'd forgotten it, but the thing is, see, *it's not him!*"

"Not him?" Maddie repeated dully. "But he looks exactly like . . . Wait a minute! The burglary! So that means that . . ."

Breaking off abruptly, Maddie turned her head as far round as she could, trying to look her mother accusingly in the eye. The bedsprings twanged beneath them.

"That means," Maddie continued, flatly, "that you have been thoroughly taken in by a man who's been impersonating someone that wasn't really Quentin Palmer in the first place!"

"I thought it was him!" Mrs Palmer croaked. "Honest, Maddie love! I thought it was him!"

There were a few seconds of cold silence.

"I don't get it," said Keith.

Before anyone could reply, the door burst open and Quentin walked into the room. In one hand he carried a bulging canvas tool bag. He let the bag fall. It landed with a shuddering crash and the sound of heavy iron tools clanking against each other.

"Well, well!" he said. "Having a family conference, are we? Can I join in? All family members welcome? Aha, but wait a minute. I don't think I can join in, can I? You see, the brutal truth is that you've all been taken for a ride! I have to tell you, and you don't know how I've been looking forward to this moment, I have to tell you all that I am not . . ."

"Yes, yes, yes!" Maddie interrupted him, scathingly, "you're not really Quentin Palmer, we worked that out ages ago!"

The man's jaw dropped. His moustache gave an involuntary twitch. He stared at Maddie for a second or two, glassy-eyed.

"Why don't you tell us something we *don't* know?"
Maddie continued. "Or, better still, why don't *we* tell
you something *you* don't know? The picture in the
silver frame that you stole from our front room,
the man with the pencil moustache and the fine cheek
bones, the person you've been posing as so
convincingly, well *he's* not Quentin Palmer either."

"What?" he said, weakly.

"No. He's . . . Who is he, Mum?"

"I don't really . . . mmm, yes. . . . know love," Mrs
Palmer said. "I cut the picture out of an old Movie
Time magazine that my mother left round here years
and years ago. He must have been some kind of
matinée idol back before the war. Ever so handsome! I
don't know what his real name was. I always called him
Quentin." As she spoke a dreamy tone began to creep
into Mrs Palmer's voice.

"But . . . surely . . . when you saw me you must have
realised?" Astonishment had robbed the man of all
emotion bar curiosity.

Mrs Palmer shook her head.

"My Quentin and me," she said, "we had a lot of
trouble. He was never much of a looker. And he was a
bit odd. Had a couple of bats loose in his belfry, my

dad used to say. I always hoped he'd change. And then . . . mmm, yes . . . when he turned up on the doorstep after all those years . . . he had!"

There was a stunned silence, broken at last by the man who was most emphatically not Quentin Palmer.

"You silly old fool!" he growled contemptuously. "What a family! I can't believe you people. You're warped, the lot of you!" He shook his head as he spoke. "Though I must admit, Madeline, I always had the nasty feeling you were one step ahead of me." He shook his head again, more violently this time. "Well, you may be clever but you're still a freak! Cooped up in this house day in and day out!" The man paused and took a deep breath.

"Well, then," he went on, "since you all know who I'm *not*, I'd better tell you who I *am*. Not my real name, of course. I'll tell you what my fellow inmates used to call me in Her Majesty's Prison, Wail Island. They used to call me . . ." he paused for effect, "Pearly White." And his teeth gleamed as he grinned his cold-eyed grin.

Maddie glared up at him. She could still hear his judgement on her ringing in her ears, "You're still a freak!" he had said. Maddie felt a surge of anger run through her.

"Pearly White?" she said with a dismissive sniff. "You sound like a dental cream for heavy smokers. Soft!" she added, unable to stop herself. "That's what your precious prison nickname makes you sound. Soft, like a smear of toothpaste!"

"I think you'll find," he said quietly, "that I'm anything but soft. I am here, in this stinking ruin you call a home, to find something. Something I intend to claim for myself. And nothing anyone can do is going to stop me." Pearly White stared at Maddie, but this time there was not even the trace of a smile on his face.

19

Pearly White paced the narrow strip of floor between the foot of the bed and the row of battered cardboard boxes stacked against the wall. The boxes contained all Mrs Palmer's clothes.

As he paced, White talked. Maddie, Keith and their mother had no choice but to listen. Maddie noticed that the bell-like tones had vanished. There was now a much harder, colder, edge to his voice.

"So. Now that we've established who we all are, after a fashion at any rate, we need to move on to the next question. How are you going to help me get what I want? As I said, and as you have probably gathered by now, Madeline, I am, indeed, looking for something. I have searched the kitchen, the front room, the under-stairs cupboard and the staircase itself. I had no need to make a search of the area below the floor because it had already been thoroughly examined by a certain . . . unwanted guest. I managed to stop him getting into the rest of the house. I'll not have anyone stop me now, not even him. Besides, if he hasn't the nerve to step in through the front door like I did, then he deserves nothing!"

On the bed, Maddie listened, her brows puckered, trying to fill in the gaps in Pearly White's increasingly rambling narrative. To her annoyance she found she could only guess at much of what he was talking about.

"As you know, I searched the ground floor myself. I examined the front room, where, yes, I had been once before, in the dead of night, with a handful of matches to light my way. The kitchen, the hallway, the cupboard under the stairs, the stairs themselves, all these places I looked at, with nothing to guide me except a piece of useless nonsense, a meaningless handful of words and numbers that I picked up in prison, which was doubtless some trick intended to throw me off the scent.

"I have taken detailed measurements of the interior walls in this house, however, and I have made an interesting discovery. The wall that divides this room from the next, the same wall that, on the ground floor, divides the kitchen from the front room, is unusually thick. It is more than double the usual thickness for such a wall. Which leads me to suspect that the wall is, in fact, hollow."

White strode to the doorway where he'd dropped his tool bag. He squatted down without taking his eyes off the Palmer family, tied up and sitting back to back on the bed. He pulled a long-handled mallet and an iron chisel from the bag and stood up, brandishing the tools.

"I don't need any meaningless notes, drivelling on about rose petals," he shouted. "All I need is a spot of elbow grease!"

So saying, he marched over to the wall and kicked aside a box brimful with wrinkled, beige coloured pop-socks. Placing his chisel dead in the centre of a wallpaper sunflower, he began to hammer away at the brickwork. After a few minutes of frenzied banging, White let out a cry of triumph. He had knocked out a brick. A cloud of orange dust floated about his head. He rammed one hand into the hole in the wall.

"I knew it!" he shouted, and shoved his hand further in. His whole arm disappeared up to the elbow. "There's a gap between these walls about a foot and a half wide!"

He snatched up the hammer and chisel once more. The hammering rang out, the skull-splitting noise bounced around the walls of the room. Maddie tried not to blink with every crack of the hammer. She found she could not help it. And she was feeling increasingly uncomfortable too. The washing line was biting into her wrists and she was getting pins and needles in her legs. She and Keith and their mother were still dressed in their nightclothes and dressing gowns and the house had grown very cold.

At last the hammering stopped. White leant back against the ravaged wall. A large hole, the size of a big television screen, had been hacked out of the brickwork. The wallpaper all around it was torn and hanging off in ragged strips.

White was wreathed in sweat. Brick dust had settled on his moustache and on his head, lending him a somewhat ginger-haired appearance.

"Now then," he said. "I have two choices. I could try to demolish this entire wall, brick by brick. But then the ceiling might collapse in on us, and I can't have that, not until I've found what I'm looking for, at least.

"So, to my other choice. I can get someone to help me. Someone that I can tie a rope around and dangle down between these two walls, someone small enough to fit into this wall cavity. Now who could that person be? Who fits the bill?"

White moved alongside the bed and looked down on his captives.

"Is it you, Madeline?" He gave a nasty laugh. "I don't think so. Or is it you, Mrs P? No. You're skinny enough, I daresay, but you don't have the brains to know what you're looking for. So it has to be you, my lad!" Pearly White lunged forward and seized Keith by the arm.

"Come, boy," he said. "It's time to dangle!"

20

"Do you see anything? Answer me, boy! Do you see anything? Just keep looking for something unusual. Something the size of a hen's egg or thereabouts. Look to your left! Hold the torch up, you little fool! OK, I'm lowering you down a bit more. Keep your elbows in, idiot child!"

The shouting went on and on. Pearly White stood at the hole in the wall, bellowing into the darkness. He played out lengths of thin nylon cord. The cord was knotted around Keith's waist. It was evidently causing him some discomfort. Every now and then his muffled voice could be heard, plaintively piping behind the brickwork.

"What's that? What's that you say?" White shouted. "The rope's cutting into your body? Ha! You'll have more than a few rope burns to worry about, my lad, if you come back up here empty-handed!"

Eventually Maddie could stand it no more.

"Bully! Child-beater! Coward!" she yelled.

At her back, Mrs Palmer voiced a protest too, for the first time, against the man she had mistaken as her husband.

"You!" said Mrs Palmer. "You . . . you . . . you . . ." her voice was trembling with rage, building in volume. White straightened, then turned to look at them.

"You . . . you . . . you . . ." Mrs Palmer spluttered on. White folded his arms and waited.

"You . . . you . . . you . . . mmm, yes . . . you . . ." Mrs Palmer, out of breath, ground to a halt and took a great gulp of air.

"Finished?" said Pearly White. "Good."

Maddie and her mother were bundled roughly out of the room, pushed across the landing and thrown into the bathroom. Without a further word, White slammed the door and left them, still tied back to back, sprawled in an undignified heap on the floor.

Maddie's face was pressed against the cold lino. She had never made such a minute inspection of the pattern; lime green with chocolate brown flecks. With a strange feeling of detachment, she decided that she did not like the pattern at all.

Maddie was much bigger than her mother, but they were around the same height. She was aware of Mrs

Palmer, flapping about somewhere behind and on top of her, uttering a series of angry squawks. The cord tying their wrists burnt and rasped against their skin. Little heels drummed into Maddie's back.

"Mum!" said Maddie, as best she could with half her mouth pressed to the floor. "Mum, can you get off me, please?"

Mrs Palmer merely squawked and flapped in an even more agitated manner. So Maddie rolled over. She heard her mother give a startled yelp and then a gasp as the wind was knocked out of her. Now lying on her side, Maddie grabbed hold of the edge of the bath and pulled herself upright. Mrs Palmer was dragged up with her. They sat back to back on the lino-covered floor, gasping for breath. They could hear Pearly White's voice echoing in the wall cavity.

"Can you see anything? Anything at all?"

"How's he expect Keith to find anything if he won't tell him what he's looking for?" Maddie muttered.

Mrs Palmer was still struggling to get her breath back.

"Oh lawks! Oh lor! Mmm, yes . . ." she gasped.

"I'm starving!" Maddie said. "What are we supposed to do for food? It's all downstairs in the kitchen and there's no way to get back down."

"Oh, lawks! Oh lor!" said Mrs Palmer, who did not seem to be listening.

"Mum," said Maddie, after a moment's pause. An idea had struck her. "The bathroom sink's made of porcelain, isn't it?"

"I'm sure I don't know!" Mrs Palmer said, who had recovered her breath at last. "Fancy thinking of a thing like that at a time like this! You and your general . . . mmm, yes . . . knowledge!"

"Yes, I'm sure it's porcelain, or something like that. So we should be able to break it. Smash it, like you'd smash a teacup, shouldn't we? I know it's a bit thicker, but it should break, shouldn't it?"

"Oh lor!" said Mrs Palmer. "She's taken leave of her senses! My poor little Maddie! She's gone clean round the bend! It's the strain of it all. Enough to push anyone over the edge. I'll be next, I know it! Mmm, yes."

"Come on, Mum," said Maddie, ignoring her mother's wailing. "On the count of three we'll both stand up. If we walk sideways we should be able to get over to the sink. Then if I can knock the toothbrush holder off the shelf it might hit the sink and chip a bit off it."

"Oh lawks!" said Mrs Palmer. "We shall both be stark,

staring bonkers inside of ten minutes, I know it for a fact!" But when her daughter counted to three and heaved herself up on her feet, she had little choice but to rise with her.

Back to back, they sidestepped over to the sink. Maddie caught sight of their reflection in the small, toothpaste-spattered mirror above the shelf. The detached part of her mind made a note of how ludicrous they looked. She told herself she might laugh about it later.

"Move over a bit, Mum!" she said, stretching out her chin, straining to reach the heavy pewter toothbrush holder on the edge of the shelf above the sink. The cold porcelain rim dug into her side as she pushed at the holder with her face. Keith's pale blue toothbrush dug into her eye but she did not stop. With one sharp jab of the chin, Maddie sent the holder skidding over the edge.

It fell like a brick, striking the side of the sink a glancing blow with a sound like the fall of a hammer. Maddie froze. Across the landing they could still hear White shouting at Keith. He did not seem to have noticed the fall of the toothbrush holder.

Maddie let out a sigh of relief. She looked down at

the sink. A piece of porcelain the size and shape of an orange segment had broken off. It looked as if someone had taken a bite out of the rim. The porcelain shard lay on the lino amongst the remains of the toothbrush holder. The three toothbrushes had scattered across the floor.

"Fantastic!" said Maddie. "It worked!"

"Stark, staring bonkers . . ." said Mrs Palmer solemnly.

21

Maddie stood on the landing, hardly daring to breathe. White had fallen silent at last. For several hours after Maddie had finally sawn through the washing line with the shard of porcelain, she and her mother had continued to sit back to back, with their arms positioned as if they were still tied together. They had expected a visit from Pearly White, but he never appeared.

The broken segment from the sink had a razor sharp edge to it. The main difficulty in cutting the cord had been getting a good grip and being able to make the right movements. White had not checked on them while they were in the midst of this painful and exhausting manoeuvre. Maddie had been able to cut through their bonds, undetected. When she had finally freed herself and her mother, she slipped the piece of porcelain into the pocket of her flannel dressing gown.

Leaving Mrs Palmer sitting on the side of the bath

still massaging her wrists even though some hours had now passed, Maddie tiptoed to the bathroom door. She opened it with infinite care, desperate to avoid any rattle of the handle or creak of the hinge, and ventured out on to the landing. Now she stood on the threshold of her mother's room, wondering why White had stopped shouting at her brother.

The door was half open. Maddie crept forward, craning to see into the room. Suddenly a snorting gurgle erupted from somewhere beyond the door. Maddie froze and clamped her hand over her mouth to stop herself crying out. With the blood pounding in her ears, she waited. As her panic subsided she realised that she had heard the noise of a man snoring.

Maddie swallowed without making a sound. She moved slowly into the room and felt the coarse texture of the bedroom carpet under her bare feet. She leaned forward and peered around the door.

Pearly White lay on the bed, the silky eiderdown pulled up to his ears. Just his hair, a wild thicket of dark, tangled locks, coated in brick dust and the residue of hair oil, was visible above the bedcovers. Sitting on the floor below the window, his wrists tied to his ankles with the same nylon cord on the end of which he had been dragged through the space between two brick walls, sat Keith.

He was looking straight at Maddie. She lifted a finger to her lips and then motioned with the flat of her hand, signalling for Keith to wait. He nodded and then gave a wan smile. His eyes, however, were wide and dark-rimmed.

Maddie stole past the bed in which White lay sleeping. He snorted alarmingly as she passed, causing Maddie to freeze; terrified that he was about to wake up. But he did not stir. After a night spent quietly demolishing a staircase and, after a brief nap, a morning passed heaving a small boy through a wall cavity on the end of a length of cord, Pearly White was clearly exhausted.

Maddie stooped and, taking the porcelain shard from her pocket, she began to saw through Keith's bonds. It was a great deal easier this time, now that she was not holding the makeshift knife behind her back and between the thumb of one hand and the little finger of the other.

The fragment of broken sink made short work of the nylon rope. Maddie wondered where this rope had come from. She knew there was a shed in the back garden, though she had never been in it. Perhaps the rope had been taken from there. She straightened up as the final knot was sawn through.

Just at that moment, White spoke from beneath the eiderdown. His voice was muffled and his speech slurred.

"No, no, no . . . the skies have cleared," he said.

The two children stood still as statues. Maddie felt a shiver of fear run through her, but she did not allow herself to tremble. She heard White turn over in bed. She dared to glance in his direction and saw that he now lay on his back, with one arm thrown over his eyes.

"No! The Mole-Hawk! Not the Mole-Hawk!" he said, still speaking in a slurred mutter. "Get away from me! Get away!"

He rolled on to his side once more and smacked his lips, sleepily. A silence fell, broken, at last, by peaceful snoring. Maddie allowed herself a silent sigh of relief. White was obviously suffering from bad dreams, but they had not been bad enough to fully wake the man. After waiting a few more minutes, just to be sure he was sleeping, Maddie and Keith crept silently out of the room.

Back in the bathroom, the three Palmers joined hands for a moment, silently acknowledging a successful start to their escape. Mrs Palmer opened her mouth as if to speak but Maddie shook her head. She was acutely aware that White could wake up at any moment. Putting one large finger to her lips she crossed to the shelf above the sink. She picked up the tube of toothpaste and knelt down beside the bath.

Squeezing a little of the white paste on to the tip of one finger, Maddie turned to the black ply-board that was fitted to the sides of the bath. She wrote on the shiny surface with her finger, the smeared white letters standing out against the dark background. Several times she paused to apply more toothpaste. The air filled with the smell of spearmint.

LOCK HIM IN! Maddie wrote.

HOW? wrote Keith.

KEY TO BEDROOM IS UNDER CARPET BY DOOR IN MY ROOM Mrs Palmer wrote, and then she added, NOW CLEAN OFF THIS MESS, MADDIE PALMER!

Maddie glared at her mother, who glared back.

LATER! MUST LOCK HIM IN NOW! Maddie wrote

in large, smudgy letters that left no room for any further additions. She stood up and headed for the door.

22

"There's something I need to check on," Maddie whispered. She had found the key where her mother had said it would be, tucked under the frayed carpet just inside the door to Mrs Palmer's bedroom – together with half a dozen flattened toffee papers and a startled earwig. And although she had locked White in, turning the key quietly in the lock, none of them wanted him to wake up before they had escaped from the upper storey of the house and summoned their neighbours to call the police. So they spoke in whispers.

"What do you need to check?" Keith mouthed the words, barely uttering a sound.

"The rose leaves," Maddie whispered back. Keith gave her a puzzled look. Mrs Palmer shook her head sadly, threw her eyes to the ceiling and tapped the side of her head with her bony index finger.

"You didn't find anything, did you, Keith?" Maddie asked.

Keith shook his head.

Maddie left him to help their mother tie knots in what was left of the washing line. The rope was thin and would be difficult to climb down. Keith insisted he could manage it. Mrs Palmer insisted on adding the knots to act as footholds.

"Can't have you breaking your neck now, Keithy love," she said, leaning forward, her voice low, "not after all this."

Maddie glided past the locked door heading for her own bedroom. A visual memory pulsed across her inner eye.

Small rose leaf – 234–13 S

And printed at the top of the sheet,

H.M. Prison: Wail Island

The grubby note she had last seen being folded into a tiny square by the man she now knew as Pearly White, was dancing through her memory, teasing and nagging at her. Rose leaves, she had realised, formed part of the patterned wallpaper in her bedroom.

Maddie's room looked just as it always had done.

There was no way of knowing, from looking at the rumpled duvet, the wicker chair and the piles of old exercise books on the floor, that the rest of the house had been plunged into chaos, with floorboards ripped up, stairs removed and parts of walls demolished.

Outside, the clouds had thinned. Weak rays of sunshine filtered into the room. Maddie stood at the foot of the bed and surveyed the walls. Drawings in pencil or black biro, drawn on the back of junk mail circulars, mostly by Maddie with one or two by Keith, covered much of the wall surface. Subjects ranged from sketches of Keith's classmates and teachers, imagined by Maddie from her brother's descriptions, to a cross section of the human eye and a sketch of the solar system recalled from a schools' TV programme.

She ignored the drawings and looked up above them, running her eyes around the wallpaper pattern close to the ceiling, counting the rose leaves.

"Two, three, four, dash, one, three," Maddie murmured under her breath, "and then there was an 'S'." She knitted her brows.

"So if we say 'S' stands for south then, well the south wall is . . ." She paused and brought to mind the direction in which the sun set, as seen from her bedroom window.

"If that way's west then the south wall is . . . this one! Now then, two hundred and thirty-four rose leaves across . . . and thirteen down."

She counted around the wall, following the pattern, stabbing the air with her forefinger, frowning with concentration.

She checked her calculations twice. Both times she found herself looking at the same place, one rose amongst a pattern containing hundreds, high up on the wall in the corner of the room.

She lifted the wicker chair and positioned it against the wall, then climbed on to it. The chair creaked and shifted under her weight. Raising her hand she felt the wall with her fingertips. There, just at the spot indicated by the pointed end of the two hundred and thirty-fourth rose leaf on the south wall, was a slightly raised area, circular in shape, about the size of a medium sized potato. Or a hen's egg.

Maddie worked her thumbnail along the edges of the raised area, tearing the wallpaper. Then she peeled it back. The paper came away easily. Underneath was a circle of tarnished metal, set into the plaster. Maddie tried pulling it out with her fingertips. She could not get a proper grip on it.

"Ow!" she said. She had slipped and bent back the nail on her middle finger. The metal circle had shifted, however. Maddie grasped the rim, now slightly protruding, between thumb and forefinger and eased it away from the wall. It seemed to be some kind of plug.

The wicker chair creaked and groaned beneath her. She shifted from foot to foot, gasping with the effort, as she tugged at the metal plug. She was dimly aware that she had abandoned her carefully observed silence. Never mind, she thought, there had been no sound from Pearly White and if he woke now he would find himself locked in Mrs Palmer's room. She would be able to escape down Keith's knotted rope before White could break the door down. Or so she hoped. Besides, she had to find out what was hidden in the wall, behind the metal plug, under the rose with the carefully recorded co-ordinates.

Maddie gritted her teeth and wiped her hand on her dress. She renewed her grip on the metal rim and pulled. At last, with a satisfying pop, the plug came away from the wall and she found herself gazing into a round hollow, half a brick deep. There was something in there, wrapped up in yellowed tissue paper.

With a trembling hand, Maddie reached in and pulled it out. The thing was heavy in her hand. She could feel its surface through the frail paper wrapping. It felt cold. With her free hand, she crumbled away the ancient tissue. She stared at the thing that lay in the palm of her hand.

It was a diamond, as big as a hen's egg. Its multi-faceted surface seemed to reflect more light than was actually in the room. It shone with the eerie appearance of intelligence. It was like an eye, looking up at her, glittering with malice and cold with contempt. Maddie shuddered. She stepped down off the wicker chair and moved back from the wall.

Then a sudden, violent hammering filled the room. Almost immediately, a large portion of wall, only a few centimetres along from where Maddie had been standing, collapsed outwards. The hefty chunk of brickwork hit the floor with a shuddering crash. Brick dust swirled around the hole that had appeared in the wall. As it cleared, Maddie could see Pearly White, leaning across a gap between the two rooms. He held a hammer in one hand and a chisel in the other. And he was smiling his gleaming white smile.

23

"Well done, Madeline Palmer!" said White. "I couldn't be more proud of you if you really *were* my own daughter. Of course, I'm going to have to ask you to hand the diamond to me. It really is far too valuable for a little girl to keep as a plaything."

He threw down the hammer and chisel and scrambled through into Maddie's room. His clothes were ripped and filthy with dirt and brick dust, his hair was wildly dishevelled and his eyes glittered like the diamond Maddie held in her hand.

"Beautiful, isn't it?" he said. "They call it the Eye of the Cyclops. It was found buried near an ancient temple on one of the Greek islands. No one knows where or when it was mined. It has passed from owner to owner since the eighteenth century, growing in price and fame each time it changed hands. A pity, in a way, that it will have to be cut into pieces. But then I could never sell it as it is. There's a woman with a pawn broker's shop in South Pridebridge who's happy to do the job, for a cut of the money I'll be making." White grinned and licked his lips.

"So, how did you find it?" he went on. "Luck? Or did you know it was here all along?" Maddie made no reply.

"Don't tell me you worked it out," he said. "What, from that piece of gibberish I got in Wail Island prison? You can hardly have got a glimpse of it! And, besides, it's just a lot of nonsense, isn't it, dreamed up to throw me off the trail?"

"I worked it out," said Maddie flatly. "I know this house."

"Yes. I expect you do," said Pearly White. He whistled through his teeth in admiration at Maddie's skills of deduction. "But," he then went on, "I'll bet you didn't know it contained such rich deposits, such buried treasures, eh? Not what you'd call a natural resource now, is it, a diamond the size of a hen's egg? How did it get here, I expect you're wondering? Well, I'll tell you. You deserve to know, since you've saved me the trouble of demolishing what's left of this hovel! It was hidden here by your father, by the *real* Quentin Palmer. The man they call the Mole-Hawk."

Out of the corner of her eye, Maddie saw the door

behind White swing open. Her mother, with Keith at her side, was standing in the doorway. She was grasping a hefty length of wood from the dismantled stairway in both hands, held up above her head. Maddie kept her eyes on White, as Mrs Palmer crept slowly towards him.

"What do you know of my father?" said Maddie. She needed to keep him talking to give her mother any kind of chance of getting close enough to hit him over the head.

"Plenty, though I've never met him," said White. "He was one of the best jewel thieves this country's ever known. He always worked alone. He tunnelled into vaults, and made his escape by flying out in a portable hang-glider he brought in with him. Hence the name, Mole-Hawk.

"He pulled off the robbery of a lifetime when he stole the Eye of the Cyclops. He got sent down for it, mind you. Twenty years on Wail Island they gave him. But no one ever found out what he'd done with the diamond. Or so they thought!"

Mrs Palmer was closing in. Keith seemed to be waiting by the door. Maddie did not dare look directly at them. She knew her eyes would give them away.

"Where did you find out about him? In prison?"

"Where else? Wail Island, Her Majesty's academy of crime! I was doing a five-year stretch for burglary. My cellmate, Jimmy the Shim, was an old acquaintance of the Mole-Hawk. The real Quentin was fool enough to trust him. Jimmy found out some pretty interesting facts about the man. He furnished me with this address for one thing. And he told me that the famous master criminal had never spent more than a few days at home in all the years of his marriage. He was always either in prison, or on the run, or working on another jewel heist. Lastly, he got me that piece of paper with the secret code on it. Three hundred rose leaves or whatever it was.

"We hatched a plan together, me and Jimmy the Shim. We were going to steal the stolen diamond, and then split the money we got for it. But I got out of prison first, didn't I?" He gave a nasty laugh.

Mrs Palmer was now standing right behind him. She raised the piece of timber high above her head. Maddie could not help herself. Her eyes flickered on to her mother for a second. White turned around with a roar. Mrs Palmer shrieked and leapt backwards. Keith ran forward and stood in front of his mother. She gripped his shoulders and stared at Pearly White, her eyes wide with fear.

White thrust his arm towards Maddie, but kept his head turned towards the mother and son, clinging together by the door.

"Give me the diamond, Madeline," said White. "Give it to me now."

"Mum!" Maddie shouted. "Catch!" She hurled the heavy diamond across the room. It struck Mrs Palmer on the forehead and bounced off. Her eyes rolled up into her head and she slipped to the floor without a sound. Pearly White caught the Eye of the Cyclops neatly in one hand.

"Thanks," he said. He pocketed the diamond and his face hardened in a look of cruel satisfaction.

But then, suddenly, his expression changed. A shadow passed before the window, momentarily blocking out the sunlight. There was a swishing sound, and the flutter of rippling canvas, just for an instant, then it was gone.

"No!" White said, and his voice cracked. "It can't be!"

24

Maddie looked at White. His face had paled beneath the brick dust smudges. His moustache twitched and trembled. Beads of sweat stood out on his forehead.

"Did you see that?" he said. "Did you see it? A hang-glider just went swooping past the window. It's him, I know it is! It's the Mole-Hawk, come back for his diamond!"

"But isn't he in prison?" said Maddie. She had no plan, now that her mother was laid out unconscious on the floor, but her instinct told her to keep the man talking, to keep on stalling him if she could.

"He must have gone under the wall!" croaked the terrified man. "He must have dug a tunnel and escaped! It was him down under the floor, trying to tunnel his way in! Now I've stopped up his rat-run, he's taken to the skies!"

"Is he really that scary?" she said.

"He's merciless!" White said. His voice was no more than a shaky whisper. "Some of the stories I've heard about him . . . they're enough to turn your hair white!"

"Well, maybe it wasn't him out there," said Maddie. "He's not the only man to own a hang-glider now, is he?"

A prolonged crash resounded above their heads, complete with the tinkle of falling glass. There was the sound of loose tiles slipping down the roof and smashing in the street below.

White gave a gasp of horror and clutched his head in his hands.

"You see!" he said. "It *is* him! I knew it!"

All eyes were turned upwards, gazing at the ceiling. All eyes except for Mrs Palmer's, that is. She was still lying on the floor, her eyelids firmly closed. The livid pink mark on her forehead had already begun to swell up into a bruise.

There was another shuddering crash from above. The ceiling shook. The cracks in the plaster widened and little clouds of dust rained down. Keith wiped his eyes with the back of his hand. Maddie turned her face away from the airborne powder. But Pearly White let the dust settle on his face without so much as a blink of the eye. He continued to stare, transfixed, up at the ceiling.

There came the sound of someone walking in the

loft. The ceiling trembled with every step. One, two, three steps. The loft was one of the few places inside the house in which Maddie had rarely set foot. She had never felt safe in the dust-scented darkness beneath the rafters, where one false step could mean falling through the ceiling of the room below in a shower of broken plaster. Nevertheless she was aware of the size of the area above their heads. She knew that three steps would take a man from the skylight to the trap-door. Sure enough, she heard the wooden door being dragged aside.

There was a brief pause, then another mighty crash. This time it was the floor that shook. Someone had jumped down out of the loft. Now they were out in the hallway, just a footstep away.

Keith backed away from the open door. Maddie swallowed. White let out a low moan and sank to his knees. A shadow fell across the doorway. A man stepped into the room.

He was dressed in the same pair of worn-looking overalls that Maddie had seen him in before, when he had climbed up out of the manhole cover in the road. He was tall and long-legged. His hands were raw skinned but surprisingly slender, with fingers like bunches of spindly carrots. His face was painfully thin, the skin stretched tightly over jutting cheekbones, the eyes deep-set and ringed with purple. There was no expression on his features, only a look of immense tiredness with perhaps a tinge of deeply ingrained sorrow.

Maddie looked into the man's eyes and recognised in them the ghost of her own gaze. Something in their depths reminded her of her reflection, looking back at her from the bathroom mirror. It was like the same eyes in a different head. And, in the outline of his temple, the curve of his skull, so clearly defined beneath the thin layer of skin and sinew, she saw the exact likeness of her brother Keith. These small but undeniable family likenesses, noticeable too, in the way the man stood, had been the cause of the nagging sense of the familiar that Maddie had felt when she saw him from her window. At the time, it had filled her with unease. But what now, now that he was here, standing in front of her? This man was her father. Here was the real Quentin Palmer, of that she could have no doubt. But what his intentions were, now that he had really returned, she had no idea.

There was no clue in his face or in his demeanour.

Without a word, he closed the door and advanced slowly into the room.

"That's close enough!" White said, scrambling to his feet. His voice was cracked, edged with desperation. "Don't come any nearer or I'll . . . I'll . . ." He stared around him, wild-eyed.

Maddie watched her father's face. He was looking at White, still impassive.

"I'm warning you!" White said.

The real Quentin Palmer raised his eyebrows a fraction. Outside, a gust of wind buffeted the house, sending another loosened tile crashing down off the roof.

Maddie could see this was the vital moment, the moment when Pearly White would either cave in and surrender or try something desperate to hold on to the jewel he had taken such pains to acquire. She kept her eyes on her father. He took another step forward.

Maddie gave a yelp of startled pain as White grabbed her wrist and dragged her across the room.

"Stay where you are, Mole-Hawk . . . Or else!" Maddie felt cold steel at her throat. White had snatched up the chisel from the floor and was pressing it against her neck.

25

"There are going to be no interruptions," White said, "no distractions, no sirens in the street. In some neighbourhoods, crashing a hang-glider into a roof might bring the police and fire brigade a-running, but not here. This is a funny town, Mole-Hawk. You've been away so long, you probably don't realise. Nobody phones the police in this town!"

Mole-Hawk did not speak. He stood perfectly still. Outside, another huge gust of wind was howling around the house. Somewhere nearby, a car alarm began to let out its high, repetitive wailing. A little further off, a dog started to bark.

"Still, I suppose the police turning up wouldn't exactly suit you, would it? You being an escaped convict on the run and all?" White gabbled on. Maddie recognised his tactics. Like she had done herself, earlier on, he was stalling for time. She could hear the desperation in his trembling, barely controlled voice.

Time moved in slow motion. The tall man in the

tattered overalls took a small but deliberate step forward. Maddie wanted to shout out to him to stop, she wanted to scream at him to do as White had asked, but the chisel at her throat kept her from making a sound. She felt him tighten his grip on her wrist, felt him draw back the blade as if to plunge it into her, but then, with a defiant shout, he flung the chisel straight at Mole-Hawk's face and shoved Maddie aside.

The tall man ducked, then straightened immediately as the chisel sailed harmlessly over his head. But White had already launched himself across the room, diving, full stretch, through the holes he had smashed in the bedroom walls. The heels of his shiny black shoes, disappearing through the jagged hole in the brickwork, were the last that was seen of him as he made his escape. For the first time, Maddie and Keith were alone with both their parents.

Mrs Palmer was still unconscious, however. She lay on the floor, limp and lifeless as an abandoned glove puppet. Mole-Hawk looked down at her in silence. Lines of sorrow were deeply etched across his features. He knelt and scooped her up in his arms. Then he carried her over to the bed, and gently laid her down again.

Meanwhile, a series of loud thuds from the next room told Maddie that White was shoulder-charging the locked door. But Mole-Hawk just stood by the bed, motionless, looking down at Mrs Palmer.

Keith was standing with his back to the wall. His eyes were wide and staring.

"Excuse me . . ." he said, in a small voice, barely more than a whisper, "excuse me, Mr Mole-Hawk . . . I think he's getting away with your diamond."

"Keith," Maddie said, "you don't have to call him Mr Mole-Hawk. He's our father. We can call him Dad."

He looked up then, and met Maddie's steady gaze. After a moment's pause, he slowly nodded his head.

"There's so much I don't understand, Dad," Maddie said. She was determined to use the word, no matter how strange it sounded. "What were you doing, digging around under the house? If you wanted the diamond, why didn't you just come and take it?"

"I was afraid the police would be watching the house," he said. His voice was soft, but with a raw edge to it. "Besides, I didn't know where Jimmy the Shim had put it. He hid it here ten years ago, just after I got sent down. Later on, I heard he went bad, but he was a good friend to me back then. And he could steal the yolk out of a nest egg without the bird sitting on it even realising it was gone. I'll bet he stowed that diamond in here without your mother knowing a thing about it."

"But why didn't you just talk to Mum? You could have got a message to her somehow. And why did you grab my hand, down under the floor," she added, accusingly, "you frightened me half to death!"

"I wasn't sure whose hand that was, Maddie. Pearly White can be a vicious man, for all his smarm. And, as for your mother, well, I was afraid . . ." Mole-Hawk's voice became choked and hesitant, "afraid I might not be welcome. After all, I've hardly been much of a husband. I never even clapped eyes on my own son until today, and I'd hardly seen much more of you, Maddie." He looked away, awkwardly. "She deserves better, your mother, much better . . ." Then he fell silent, his sorrowful gaze fixed once again on the recumbent form of Mrs Palmer.

A splintering crack and a cry of triumph from next door told them that White had succeeded in smashing his way out on to the landing.

"The diamond!" Keith hissed urgently. He was a boy with a marked sense of justice. White's plan to cheat his way to the hidden gem had clearly touched a raw nerve, and he was convinced that the diamond belonged, by rights, to his father, despite the fact that Mole-Hawk had stolen it himself in the first place.

"Yes," Mole-Hawk tore his eyes away from the bed, "yes, you're right! I must get the diamond. Then, at least, I can keep you all in the manner you deserve. I've been sending your mother enough to get by on, a cheque in the post each month, she probably thinks it's from the Social Security or something. But with that diamond I could give you a new home, a new life!"

"Hurry!" Keith said. "He's getting up into the loft, I can hear him!"

Mole-Hawk moved towards the door, then looked back one last time.

"You always deserved something better," he said, speaking to the unconscious Mrs Palmer. "You should have got the man of your dreams. Film star looks, gin and tonics, everything!" He turned to Maddie and Keith, standing awkwardly at the bedside.

"She's an angel, your mum is," he said. "Take care of her for me, there's good kids. Sorry I never got to know you two." With that, he strode across the room and threw open the door.

Looking past him, out on to the landing, Maddie saw a pair of shiny black shoes disappearing through the trapdoor into the loft. White had found the stepladder in its place behind the boiler in the bathroom. Now it stood on the landing, rocking slightly on its uneven legs.

"An angel?" Keith said. Both children looked at their mother lying on the bed, wrapped in her plaid woollen dressing gown, a crumpled tissue handkerchief hanging out of one of the pockets, her eyes tightly closed and her mouth half open. Maddie turned to Keith and shrugged.

They both looked up when they heard the thud of footsteps on the rafters above. Once again, dust began to seep through the cracks in the ceiling as two pairs of feet made their way across the loft to the skylight.

"Keith, I need to see what's going on," said Maddie.

"No, Maddie," her brother said. "It's dangerous." He paused then added, "*They're* dangerous!"

"Don't worry, I'm just going to watch what happens," said Maddie. "I'll be careful."

"But if he tries to escape in the hang-glider . . ." Keith bit his lip. "Listen to the wind!" he said.

Outside the wind was indeed gusting with

frightening strength. More car alarms had been set off, more dogs were barking, and tiles could be heard being blown off rooftops all down the street.

But then the weather outside became just an unnoticed background again as they heard the unmistakable sounds of a violent struggle from up in the loft.

Maddie hurried out on to the landing. She clambered up the stepladder. By standing crouched on the very top step, she was able to reach up and grab on to the frame of the trapdoor opening. She stood up, and felt the stepladder wobble alarmingly beneath her feet. Just as Maddie's head and shoulders rose up through the trapdoor and into the loft, the ladder lurched to one side and was suddenly gone. Gripping desperately to the rough timber of the trapdoor's frame, Maddie kicked at thin air. She heard Keith shout her name and the crash as the stepladder hit the floor.

26

Thoughts flickered through Maddie's consciousness, all in the few brief seconds during which she hung there, dangling from the loft trapdoor, struggling to support her own weight. If she let go, Maddie thought, she would probably hit the balustrade. The railing would either break, or it would momentarily, and very painfully, break her fall. Either way she would still end up being pitched headfirst into the space where the stairs used to be. She pictured herself, a broken, if rather large, doll, sprawled on the floor of what had once been the understairs cupboard.

Almost before these thoughts had formed, Maddie realised that she could not hope to hold on. She looked up, her teeth bared in a grimace of pain and alarm. There was the shattered skylight. Daylight spilled through on to the rafters. Mole-Hawk must have broken the glass to get into the loft. There was no sign of either man.

Then Mole-Hawk's face suddenly appeared,

contorted with agony, framed by the damaged skylight. Maddie, her fingers just beginning to lose their grip, saw his expression change. Worried concern added itself to his grimace of exertion as he noticed her plight. With a cry of pain he dragged himself in through the skylight, headfirst.

He plummeted down towards her. Maddie screamed. But a rope that he had wound around his upper arm and waist checked his fall. He hung upside down, like a bungee jumper, suspended just above the trapdoor opening. There was a yell from somewhere behind him and the loft seemed to darken, but Maddie could no longer see anything except Mole-Hawk, hanging just above her.

"I'm going to fall!" she gasped.

Mole-Hawk shook his head.

"No," he said, "you're not."

He reached down and took hold of her arms below the elbow. Immediately her hands slipped from the frame.

For one frightening moment she felt her weight pulling her father down through the trapdoor. Then Maddie felt the stepladder beneath her feet. Keith had managed to set it back up. Maddie saw Mole-Hawk look past her and give her brother a nod of approval.

"That fool's trying to launch the hang-glider!" Mole-Hawk's voice was hoarse and breathless. He was bracing himself against a mighty tugging on the rope around his arm. "He's no pilot. He'd break his neck in perfect weather conditions, let alone in this storm!" He gritted his teeth and yanked down on the rope with both hands. "But I . . . have . . . the end of the tethering rope!" he grunted, struggling hard to maintain his hold.

Maddie could see past his shoulder now. The red fabric wing of the glider was covering the skylight. The loft was filled with a gloomy, red-tinged light, broken here and there by brighter sunbeams wherever a tile was missing from the roof. White's head and upper body were visible, hanging down through the skylight. He was all tangled up in the hang-glider harness and was frantically pulling at the tethering rope with both hands.

The moaning of the wind suddenly rose to a frenzied roar. The gale filled the loft, heaving at the rafters. Timbers groaned alarmingly and more gaps appeared in the tiles. Maddie's hair was blown about her face, blinding her for an instant. When she clawed the strands away from her eyes, Mole-Hawk and White had vanished.

"Hold the ladder, Keith!" Maddie shouted.

"I am!" Keith said, his voice sounding very far away. Maddie pushed against the stepladder and, taking hold of one of the roof beams, pulled herself up into the loft.

She hesitated when she saw the gaping skylight, with no glass to shield her from the vastness of the sky. But she had to know what was happening. She had to look outside. Covering her head with her hands, Maddie forced herself to cross the loft.

By the time she reached the skylight, Mole-Hawk and White were already fifty metres up in the air. The heavily gusting wind had scooped up the hang-glider, with White half strapped into it, and sent it soaring skywards. Mole-Hawk, with the tethering rope still wound tightly about his arm and waist, had been dragged up behind it, out through the skylight and into the ether.

Maddie watched them, transfixed. The glider was tossed higher and higher, as helpless as a leaf caught in an autumn storm. White, clinging to the flimsy frame and Mole-Hawk, trailing behind on a length of rope, buffeted this way and that, looked like a pair of hapless dolls, tied to a kite by an evil-minded child and then released into the teeth of a gale.

Keith joined Maddie at the skylight. They both watched the hang-glider, now a tiny red triangle high in the air, soaring over Pridebridge town. Then Keith gave a gasp of horror as the fickle wind now sent the glider hurtling downwards, only to snatch it up again just as it disappeared from sight behind a row of tall buildings.

"They're over the river!" Keith shouted. "Maybe if they crash in the water they won't be hurt!"

Maddie watched, her emotions numb. Pearly White had brought them nothing but anxiety and ultimately fear. There was no reason to hope for a safe landing for him. And yet, to see a man plummet to his death in front of your eyes was horrifying, whoever he was. And what of Mole-Hawk, suspended beneath the stricken glider like a sky-diver with a faulty parachute? He was a thief and a convict, but he was also their real father. Maddie gripped the skylight frame until her knuckles turned white.

The hang-glider reappeared, plucked upwards once more, spinning in a spiralling eddy of winds, a miniature tornado at the heart of the storm. It hung for a moment, high above the River Pride. Maddie saw a tiny flash of light, no more than a pinpoint, but shimmering bright as a flame. It detached itself from the glider and fell through the air, glittering in the sunlight that was streaming through the ragged clouds, as it plunged towards the river below.

"Keith," she said, "did you see that?"

"The diamond!" breathed Keith.

Then the wind caught the glider's tattered wings once more and carried it high. Up and up it spun, until the two figures attached to it were too tiny to distinguish, and the glider itself was no more than a speck of red against the boiling grey clouds. Then it was lost, disappearing into a mass of scudding vapour. When the clouds parted again, the glider was nowhere to be seen.

That was the last Maddie saw of the red hang-glider. And it was the last she saw of her two fathers, one false and the other true, both of them gone.

It was later that day, as they wandered about their ruined home, after first clambering down the knotted washing line to prepare a welcome meal of bread and peanut butter, that Mrs Palmer finally regained consciousness and made them swear to keep the whole episode a secret.

"I don't want to talk about it!" she told her children. "Not now, not never! I want it to be like it never ever happened! Mmm, yes."

And so Mrs Palmer told the astonished workmen who came to repair the house that the damage had all been caused by the storm, and, although none believed her, she stuck resolutely to the story. For Maddie and Keith, those traumatic few days became a taboo subject, and then, as the months turned to years, a buried memory, sealed up like a locked room in an old deserted house.

Until now.

Maddie sat back. Grandad Lemon let out a low whistle. Water slopped against the side of the old riverboat.

"Well," Grandad said at last, "I knew your mother was something of an eccentric, but, blimey . . .!" He whistled again, and scratched his chin through his wispy white beard.

"She's been out on deck all night," Keith said, quietly.

"Look," said Maddie, pointing at the porthole, "it's getting light. It's morning."

All three of them went out, the old man watching awkwardly from the wheel-house door as Maddie and Keith went and stood on either side of their mother, taking hold of a hand each.

"Where did you put the baked beans, Mum?" said Maddie.

"I slung them in the river," said Mrs Palmer, "saucepan and all."

"That's all right," Maddie said, "we can have eggs for breakfast instead."

They watched the dawn breaking over the river. Coots and moorhens paddled across the silver surface of the water. A heron glided down over the reed-beds and landed in the shallows with barely a splash.

"Grandad," Maddie said, "we're heading downstream, aren't we?"

"Downstream," he nodded, "towards the sea."

Maddie thought of the diamond, the Cyclops's eye. She wondered if the pull of the river had dragged it downstream. She pictured it, rolling through the silt-covered riverbed, its glittering surfaces dulled in the green, underwater light. In three years it might have got this far. It could now be under the bows of *The Pridebridge Princess*, just a dozen feet of dirty water away from where they were all standing.

Maddie went to bed. While she slept, she dreamed. In her dream, she stood on a rope bridge, suspended high up above a jungle pass. Below the bridge Maddie could see the whole world spread out beneath her: rivers, oceans, mountain ranges, deserts and snowfields, great cities and wide empty plains. Close by, lying asleep on the bridge, was her mother. Maddie could hear her gentle snoring.

"An angel!" said a voice.

"Yes," said Maddie, agreeing happily, "she's an angel!"

She leaned out over the bridge, which swayed dangerously.

"I'm going to fall!" Maddie said, suddenly afraid.

"No," said her father, "you're not." And her fear faded away.

Maddie awoke from the dream smiling. Sunlight was streaming in through the cabin porthole. A new day had already begun.